D0986336

indigo
girl

indigo girl

SUZANNE KAMATA

GEMMA

BOSTON

First published by GemmaMedia in 2019.

GemmaMedia
230 Commercial Street
Boston, MA 02109 USA

www.gemmamedia.com

Printed in the United States of America

19 20 21 22   1 2 3 4

978-1-936846-73-3

Library of Congress Cataloging-in-Publication Data

Names: Kamata, Suzanne, 1965—author.
Title: Indigo girl / Suzanne Kamata.
Description: Boston : GemmaMedia, 2019. | Summary: Fifteen-year-old Aiko Cassidy, a manga enthusiast with cerebral palsy, spends a summer in Japan,m learning about her father's family and making new friends, while avoiding her stepfather and baby half-sister.
Identifiers: LCCN 2019005490 | ISBN 9781936846733
Subjects: | CYAC: Americans—Japan—Fiction. | Racially mixed people—Fiction. | Cerebral palsy—Fiction. | People with disabilities—Fiction. | Remarriage—Fiction. | Family life—Japan—Fiction. | Japan—Fiction.
Classification: LCC PZ7.K12668 Ind 2019 | DDC [Fic]—dc23 LC record available at https://lccn.loc.gov/2019005490

Cover design: Laura Shaw Design

*This book is dedicated to the survivors of
the triple disaster which struck Northeastern
Japan on March 11, 2011.*

1

Six hours and counting down till Father's Day, and I've got nothing. Mom brought me along with her to Walmart so I can pick out a gift or a greeting card. With my good hand, I reach for a card from the rack and flip it open: *So many memories we've built together* . . . No. Too early for that. I pick up another. On the front, there's a cartoon picture of a blond guy with blue eyes. Nope, not that one either. Raoul has dark hair. *To the world's greatest dad!* Umm . . . considering all of the times over the past year I've lashed out with "You're not my real father!" that one would seem totally fake.

It's not that Raoul is a bad person. As stepfathers go, I'd say he's in the ninetieth percentile. But it's been hard getting used to living with a guy after fifteen years in a testosterone-free zone. Mom didn't marry my real father, who lives in Japan (who I will be spending time with very, very soon!), so it's always been just the two of us.

My best friend, Whitney, tried to prepare me. Her parents are divorced, and she lives with her mother, but she has an older brother. "Guys always leave the toilet seat up," she warned me. "And there will be dirty socks all over the place."

Well, she was wrong about that. While Mom is of the "messiness is a sign of creativity" school of thought, Raoul is a neat freak. As soon as he moved in, he was on us about the drifts of unopened mail and school memos that seemed to build organically on one end of the dining room table. He didn't understand why there were always socks missing when we sorted the laundry. And it drove him mad when we left empty mugs in the living room instead of bringing them to the sink.

"Clutter hurts the brain," he told me once. "It's been scientifically proven."

Raoul is not a scientist. He's a musician. He listens to music while he cleans. He hums as he does the dishes. He can compose without making a mess.

Mom and I can't vacuum while we sculpt and draw. That's just the way it is. There's hardly enough time in the day after school (for me) and teaching (for Mom) to make art. If the question is whether to declutter or draw, the answer is clear. Which is not to say that I like clutter. In fact, it's nice to live in a tidy house with a well-stocked fridge and matched socks. And he's a fabulous cook. It's nice for Mom and me to have someone to help with my homework and with paying the bills and taking out the garbage, but sometimes I miss just hanging out with Mom and eating ice cream for supper while watching some chick flick in our underwear.

I give up on the cards and drift over to aisle four to take a look at the kitchen gadgets, humming along with the Muzak as I go. Does Raoul have a cherry pitter? I wonder. Yeah, probably. His toolbox is filled with just about everything you could imagine. The man even has a spring-loaded ravioli stamp.

"Did you find something?" Mom comes up behind me, pushing a cart heaping with disposable diapers and groceries.

"No," I admit. "I'm new at this."

She smiles and squeezes my shoulder. "Why don't you make a card?"

"Yeah, maybe." My wedding gift for Mom and Raoul last year was an original manga love story set in Paris. They both adored it—Mom went on and on about my "strong lines" and "perspective" and Raoul raved about the scene where Gadget Girl and The Kitchen Musician rappel down the Eiffel Tower—but it took a long time to draw. I've only got a few hours till the big day.

"Well, we'd better get going. It's almost time for Esme's dinner." Mom glances down at her chambray shirt, checking for milk leaks.

"Okay." I follow her as she goes through the checkout line and trail her and the bag boy pushing our cartload of groceries. Just before we shove through the glass doors into the gathering dusk, I hear a kid say, "Why's that girl walking so funny? What's wrong with her?"

Mom freezes, and I know she's thinking about stopping and talking to the little boy. *Here is a teachable moment.* It's a habit—one that she's trying hard to break now that at fifteen-going-on-sixteen I'm plenty old enough to speak up for myself.

I have cerebral palsy. As far as I'm concerned, why I limp is nobody's business, but I turn to the kid all the same. He's about five—shaggy-haired and snaggletoothed, wearing jeans and a T-shirt advertising some band that he's too young to be listening to.

I smile at the kid and at his mom, a plus-size lady in a tent dress.

"There's nothing wrong with me," I say. "Nothing at all."

They're too stunned or confused to respond, but Mom gives me a little smirk, her sign of approval. Then she drapes her arm over my shoulder, and we walk all the way out to the car.

At home, we can hear the baby squalling as soon as Mom opens the car door. Esme is quite the screamer.

We hurry into the house, where Raoul is pacing the living room with my baby sister against his shoulder. His face lights up as soon as he sees us.

"How long has she been crying?" Mom asks.

"Oh, not long," Raoul says good-naturedly. "Only about an hour."

Crying is good. Or at least it's better than not being able to cry. I was born fourteen weeks too early, before my lungs had finished developing. I spent months in the NICU with a tiny tube down my throat. I couldn't get out a sound until much later. Mom doesn't mind so much when Esme cries, though to me she seems unhappy. I'd rather make her giggle. I tickle her perfect tiny feet, but she keeps on crying.

Mom holds out her arms for the baby. The two of them settle in an armchair, and Esme immediately quiets down. Raoul sits down on the floor beside them. They look so perfect together. They look like a family. And they *are* a family—the Rodriguez family. I'm Aiko Cassidy, the odd one out.

I slip out of the room, leaving them to their bliss. They don't even seem to notice.

Well, pretty soon I'll be out of here. Two more weeks and I'll be back where I belong, if only for the summer—land of Ghibli and iced matcha lattes, land of indigo and cat cafes and manga and J-pop. I'll be in the country where I was born, where, with my distinctly Asian features I will look like everybody else, unlike here where I'm surrounded by flaxen-haired daughters of Dutch descendants.

Meanwhile, there are five hours and thirteen minutes to go till Father's Day and I'm still stumped. I close myself in my room and sketch for a while, which is what I do when I need to calm down. My pencil starts to outline my manga character, Gadget Girl, almost automatically. Sometimes ideas come to me on the page as if they are channeled from Creativity Central, but this time it doesn't work. Gadget Girl just stares at me, doing nothing. About half an hour later, I bring my best friend Whitney up on Skype.

"Help! I need some advice."

Whitney's face, all covered with white paste, looms onto the screen. Her frizzy dark hair is bundled into a towel. "That's what I'm here for," she says. "What's the problem?"

"I'm not sure what to do about tomorrow. You know, Father's Day? What kind of gift is appropriate? What should I write on the card? I don't even know what to call him."

"Well," Whitney's eyes go up, as if she'll find the answer on the ceiling. "How do you feel about him? Do you love him? Do you feel like saying 'I love you' when you see him at the breakfast table?"

I shrug. "I think he's a really great guy. I'm not

sure that I'm ready to start calling him 'Dad,' though. What are you giving your father?"

"Nate and I chipped in on a Weber grill. Something small for camping so we can at least cook our food if we're forced to go on another deprivation vacation."

I laugh. It's a good gift, but I can't imagine Mom and Raoul in the woods, especially not since Esme has come along. They're more hotel people.

"Hey," Whitney says. "What about your other dad?"

I shrug. "I don't even know if they celebrate Father's Day in Japan."

Whitney rolls her eyes. "Excuses, excuses. Ever heard of Google?"

Okay, okay. It would have been easy enough to look into but I don't know how I feel about my real father, either. For fourteen years, I had no contact with him. I didn't even know who he was. When Mom finally told me, under duress, I got in touch. Now we talk via Skype a couple of times a month, but I don't think we've reached the hugs and kisses stage yet.

"Maybe next year," I say. "We'll see how this summer goes." I'll be spending my summer vacation with my biological father and his family for the first time ever. Mom knows that I've wanted to visit Japan for, like, forever, and she's totally in support of the visit, even though she could probably use some extra help with Esme.

"So you *are* going," Whitney says.

"Yeah. He says it's safe."

Since the huge earthquake last spring, and the devastating tsunami, and the meltdown at the nuclear power plant, everyone around here thinks Japan is one big disaster zone. My brother Junpei—my half brother, that is—assures me that everything is fine in Shikoku where they live. It's hundreds of miles from the devastated area.

This might sound odd, but after watching footage of the tsunami on YouTube and reading about the damage and all of money raised by American celebrities to aid Japan, I wanted to go there even more than before. I felt like I should be there in solidarity, doing something to help.

"Well, maybe you should wait till next year to celebrate with Raoul, too," Whitney suggests. "Wait till it feels right. Then you'll know what to do. You'll be able to think of the perfect gift."

"Yeah, you might have a point."

I set my alarm before I go to bed. I've decided that I'll get up early and go to mass with Raoul. He'll like that. He usually has to go alone. I'm not Catholic, and neither is Mom, but recently I've become really interested in the saints, such as St. Thomas Kozaki, a fifteen-year-old Japanese boy who was crucified in sixteenth-century Nagasaki for his beliefs. Or St. Elizabeth of Hungary, the patron saint of bakers, countesses, the homeless, and the falsely accused. Or Clare of Assisi, the patron saint of television. I also like the rituals of the service, the incense, the recitations.

When I stumble into the kitchen, Raoul's just sitting down with a cup of coffee, all dressed for church in an earth-toned blazer and tie. Sunlight streams in through the window. A robin perched in the lilac bush just outside twitters a song. I'm wearing my favorite indigo dress, the one with the scalloped neckline.

"Hey! Where are you going looking like that?" he asks, spooning sugar into his coffee.

"I thought I'd go with you," I say. "Keep you company."

The rest of the house is quiet, except for the ticking of a clock. Mom and Esme are still asleep.

His eyes glisten, and I realize I've moved him to tears. "I'd like that," he says.

Before the service begins, the congregation is supposed to greet each other. I stand up alongside Raoul, who nodded at just about everyone we passed on the way to our pew. The white-haired couple in front of us turns and smiles. I don't think I've ever met them before, but they seem to know him.

Suzanne Kamata

The wife takes both of his hands in hers. "Good morning, Raoul!" Her eyes flicker to me.

"This is Aiko," he says. "My oldest daughter."

They study me for a moment, as if they're trying to figure out how a girl with a Hispanic dad and white mom ended up with Asian features.

"Actually, stepdaughter," I put in helpfully. "My real dad is in Japan."

The light fades from Raoul's eyes, and I realize that I've hurt his feelings, but he manages a stiff smile. "Aiko, meet Mr. and Mrs. Vanderpool."

I thrust out my right hand. My left hand is stiff and curled and tucked into a pocket. Mrs. Vanderpool reaches out two blue-veined hands, heavy with rings. I see confusion dance across her face as she notices that I am withholding my other hand, but she quickly recovers and smiles. "We're so happy to have you here with us this morning," she says to me. And to Raoul, "What a lovely young lady!"

When we get back from church, Mom has brunch all laid out, which is kind of surprising. Before Raoul, we ate a lot of cold cereal. Today, however, the table is covered with white damask and there are plates of blueberry muffins, eggs scrambled with mushrooms and peppers, and a big bowl of fruit salad. It all looks delicious.

Mom looks good, too. She's wearing a dress printed with roses. Esme is cradled in her arms.

"Hey, sis," I say, dropping a kiss on her downy head.

She smells clean and fresh. Her fingers flutter, grasping at my hair.

"Wow, Mom. I didn't know you could cook," I say.

"Ha, ha. Very funny." She hands Esme over to Raoul. "Happy Father's Day, honey."

We all sit down at the table. When we're halfway through our meal, Mom hauls out the presents: a striped apron, a CD of Tibetan folk tunes, and a small painting.

"Can I see?" I ask.

Raoul admires the painting for a few seconds more before handing it over to me. It's of him, holding a baby. Mom has managed to fill the small canvas with a father's adoration. The look in his eyes is pure love. His arms encircle the baby and hold her close. She looks safe, cherished. The plump, pink infant is Esme, of course. It brings to mind all of the paintings of the Madonna and Child that we saw at the Louvre last summer, except with the genders reversed. That's the idea. Mom wants to get people thinking about fathers and children. She's also working on a sculpture of Raoul and Esme.

"It turned out well," I say. I feel a flicker of jealousy.

For a long time I wanted Mom to paint anything but me, so I should be glad she's found another subject. Up until a little over a year ago I was her main muse, but then I asked her to stop using me as her model. She agreed, saying that with my talent I was better off representing myself. Not that I feel compelled to plaster my image all over everything. I'm not into self-portraits. I'd rather draw the characters that pop up in my imagination.

Mom looks from me to Raoul and back again.

I squirm a little, knowing what's expected of me. "Happy Father's Day, Raoul," I say shyly. I've decided that I'm not even going to say anything about a gift, or the lack of one.

The words seem to please him, though. Not quite a Weber grill, but maybe it's enough.

Back when Mom and Raoul first got married he offered to adopt me, but it didn't feel right. It seemed too early. I thought we should develop more of a father-daughter relationship before we made it official. Also, I wanted to get to know my biological dad first. Now I wonder if Raoul still thinks about adopting me. Maybe he's given up or forgotten about it. He has a daughter of his own, after all—Esme. It could be that I've lost my chance.

2

One thing Mom and Raoul don't understand about our house is that sound carries through the register in my room. When I'm lying in bed later that night, I listen to them talking in the living room. I can make out every word.

"I'm so worried that this summer will be a disappointment. I can't imagine them treating her like one of the family after all this time. If he didn't want her then, why would he want her now?"

Mom's words make my skin break out in goose bumps. They're obviously talking about me. They're worried that my real father will reject me again, that he'll turn out to be a world-class jerk and I'll have my heart broken. I've met him, though. We've talked via webcam and he seems like a pretty nice guy. During one of our first conversations, he told me that he was sorry, and he had tears in his eyes. He's making an effort. He's invited me to live with his family for three months! I want to throw off the covers, storm into the living room, and defend him. If I did that, though, Mom and Raoul would know that I can hear them, and I'd never be able to eavesdrop again.

Instead, I roll back my quilt, turn on my computer, and compose an e-mail message: *Happy Father's Day, Otosan! I can't wait to see you in two weeks! Love, your daughter, Aiko.* I hit send.

When I wake up the next morning, I check my inbox, but there's no reply. Now I'm wondering if it was such a good idea to send such a mushy greeting. I've sent him a few e-mails up till now, but I've never signed off with "love" or "your daughter." And he's never signed his messages with "love" or "your dad." From what I understand, the Japanese are not super demonstrative. Maybe I embarrassed him.

I pull on a pair of shorts and a T-shirt and go out to the kitchen. Raoul is already there, with baby Esme over his shoulder. Both he and Mom teach at the community college in Muskegon. Now that it's summer vacation, they don't have to go to work. Of course, they're busy with their projects—Mom with her sculptures, and Raoul with his music.

I have my project, too. I am the creator of *Gadget Girl*, a manga series about a girl who wields gadgets like eggbeaters and Swiss Army knives with extreme precision and skill in order to save people from marauding jackrabbits, snow golems, and other sorts of evil. I have fans all over the world. But I'm in a slump. I've run out of ideas. I'm hoping that this summer's trip to Japan will change that. I figure that when you visit a foreign country, the smallest of things can turn into an interesting story. There should be plenty to write about.

"Would you mind watching the baby for a couple hours this morning?" Raoul asks me now, here in the kitchen. "Your mom wants me to pose for her."

"Sure, I'll keep an eye on Esme." My other project is helping with my sister.

"But you need some breakfast first," Raoul says. "How about a smoothie?"

"That sounds great."

I settle in my chair and he hands the baby over. With my elbow on the armrest and Esme's head pillowed in the crook of my right arm, we're both feeling secure. She looks up at me with her pool-blue eyes and makes a gurgling sound.

"Don't forget about me while I'm gone, okay?" I tell her. "Remember this face."

"We'll plaster the side of her crib with photos of you," Raoul jokes. He chops up an avocado and a banana and tosses them into the blender.

"And maybe you'd better record my voice, too," I say. "I can sing some lullabies."

The truth is that even though Esme wakes me up with her middle-of-the-night squalls, and she spits up all over my clothes, and takes up a lot of Mom's and Raoul's—and my—time, I'm crazy about her. I think she likes me, too. But she's little. She'll forget me. I imagine that over the summer Mom, Raoul, and Esme will hardly notice that I'm gone. They'll bond as a happy little family unit, and I'll no longer fit in at all. As much as I'm looking forward to going to Japan, the thought of losing my place here makes me almost want to stay.

When Raoul starts up the blender, Esme starts to fuss, so I make a clucking noise and jiggle my arm a little. That seems to calm her down.

"Here you are, my dear." Raoul sets a glass in front of me. "I'll stick your sister in the bouncy chair while you drink this." He scoops her up, kisses the top of her head, and heads off to Mom's studio.

I like that he trusts me with Esme. Sometimes *I* worry that I'll drop her or something, but it never seems to cross his mind.

3

The day before I leave for Japan, Whitney comes over to help me pack. I've pretty much mastered folding clothes with one hand, but things go faster with another person.

My pink suitcase is splayed open on my bed, like a big hungry mouth. A pile of clothes and other stuff I want to take are heaped next to it.

Whitney grabs a T-shirt and holds it up. "Tulip Festival, Holland, Michigan," she says, reading the words printed on white cotton. A giant pair of wooden shoes surrounded by tulips in various colors takes up the rest of the space. "Is this new? I've never seen you wear this before."

I shrug. "I heard that there's this fake Dutch village in Nagasaki. I thought I could wear it if we went there. You know, ironically."

She folds it neatly and lays it at the bottom of my suitcase.

"And this?" she says, picking up a long blue wig.

"Seriously? Aren't you going to the countryside? To a farm?"

"Junpei says that they do cosplay in Tokushima. There's a festival every summer."

"Alrighty, then." She smooths out the strands and settles it on top of the T-shirt.

"Your bio-dad has WiFi, right?" she asks.

"Yeah, I guess. Japan's a pretty modern country," I deadpan. I've never asked, but as far as I can tell, my father's house is fully wired.

"I mean, you'll be able to check your e-mail, won't you? In case I need advice on the Luke situation."

I roll my eyes. I'm the last person she should be asking about relationships. I've never had a boyfriend before.

"So have you heard from your French lover boy?" she asks me.

The only guy I've ever gone out with is Hervé, the guy I met last summer when Mom and I went to Paris. We rode around on his scooter, seeing the sights. He translated *Gadget Girl* into French and once, right before I was about to get on the plane to come home, he kissed me. Ooh la la!

"According to his Facebook status he is currently 'in a relationship,'" I say. "With Celeste."

He has this on-again off-again girlfriend, Celeste. Last summer they were conveniently off.

"Oh. Too bad," Whitney says. "I bet you'll meet some hot guy in Japan."

"I'm not going over there to meet guys. I'm going so I can get to know my Japanese family. And I want to really try to fit in and learn the language, so I'm not going to be texting America all the time, okay?"

Her shoulders sag. So maybe my tone was a little snippy.

"But if there's an emergency, I'll be there for you," I add quickly.

Lately, Luke has been putting pressure on her to move their relationship to the next level. They've been together for a year now, and they're still both virgins. Whitney isn't ready to go further, though, and it's created some tension between them. Of course, as her best friend I hear about this ad nauseum.

To be completely honest, I'm looking forward to taking a break from the Whitney-and-Luke drama-rama. I'm looking forward to not feeling like the third wheel as they feed each other Cheetos in the school cafeteria and act out entire scenes from old movies. Although I admit that it's been an education. If I wind up on some crazy quiz show in Japan, I'll be able to answer all of the questions about *Casablanca*.

Before I go to bed, I grab my guidebook to Japan and do some last-minute cramming: "I'm sorry" is "*gomenasai.*" No shoes in the house. No soap in the bathtub. Don't leave chopsticks standing up in a bowl of rice. "Excuse me" is "*sumimasen.*" The number for emergencies is 119.

I double-check my suitcase to make sure I remembered to tuck in my special slippers and my phone charger. My body is all buzzy with anticipation and I'm pretty sure I won't sleep a wink, but then one minute I'm staring through a gap in the curtains at the constellations, and the next I'm deep in a dream hanging out with Luffy, the pirate in the manga *One Piece*. And then my alarm clock goes off and it's finally time to get up and go.

4

I'm in the sky. Here above the clouds, I'm in limbo: between America and Japan, between the past and the future. It's weird, but for once I feel as if I'm where I belong. Right now, at this very moment, I don't have to choose between names or countries or fathers.

But then the plane begins its descent and my ears start to pop. Outside, I see the sprawling city of Osaka and the blue bay. At first I think we're not going to make it to the landing strip. The sea looks as if it's rising up to meet us. I take note of the exit sign and feel under my seat for the life jacket.

I close my eyes and take a deep breath. The wheels of the plane bump down onto the runway. I'm here. I'm finally in Japan.

I follow the other passengers off the plane and through immigration, where I have to leave impressions of my fingerprints and irises, and then we go up an escalator then down some stairs to the baggage claim.

Everything seems cleaner and more orderly here than at the airport in Detroit. No one is speaking loudly. No one is rushing or shoving.

I watch the suitcases go by on the carousel—the monogrammed Louis Vuitton bags and the look-alike black ones—until my pink suitcase, the one Mom gave me for my birthday last year, pops into view.

I heave it off the conveyor belt and onto a luggage cart. I show my passport one last time and finally exit through automatic doors to the arrivals lounge.

The first thing I see is a wall of Japanese people holding signs. I don't really expect to find my name on a piece of cardboard. I mean, we've met on Skype. They've seen my picture; they know what I look like, and vice versa. But there it is: "Welcome, Aiko!" Written in indigo-blue ink.

Junpei is holding the sign. He's taller than I expected, and lankier. He smiles shyly and nods when he sees me. Next to him is a man—my father—and a woman with straight black hair cut in a chic asymmetrical bob, wearing a floaty dress tie-dyed in indigo. She doesn't look like a farmer's wife.

We just stare at each other for a second, unsure of ourselves. Did I imagine that my father would embrace me, his long-lost daughter? Or that he'd start crying into my neck, like Mom in Detroit? No one around us is hugging. It's not that kind of place.

Finally, he holds out his hand for a shake. I notice that it's tinged with the blue dye from the indigo vats. Even though I'd been warned about it, the effect is unsettling. His hands are like zombie hands or the hands of someone with some weird skin disease. Still, when I reach out, his grasp is surprisingly warm and not at all clammy like mine.

Next my father's wife, Mariko, steps forward and bows to me. "I hope you had a good flight," she says carefully. "Obaachan is waiting for us at home."

Ah, Obaachan. *The grandmonster.* Or at least that's what I'd grown up believing—that my Japanese grandmother was shrivel-hearted and mean, that she drove my mother away and kept my parents apart.

"Shall we go?" my father says, gesturing toward the doors.

Junpei grabs my suitcase without being told, and I follow along behind my father. As I stare at his narrow shoulders and his thinning hair, I wonder what Mom ever saw in him. He doesn't have Raoul's energy or the take-charge attitude of Rolfe, the foreign correspondent boyfriend before him. Her type must have changed drastically.

Even the car he directs me into, a standard black four-door sedan, is pretty staid and boring compared to Raoul's convertible. I climb into the back seat with Junpei while my father puts my suitcase into the trunk.

Off to the left is the sparkling sea, the same sea that rose up and swallowed entire villages farther north. Today it looks calm, benevolent. The city of Osaka, one of the largest cities in the world, sprawls on the left. The elevated highway takes us past apartment buildings and gleaming towers with helipads and Universal Studios Japan.

"That's Koshien," my father says, indicating a baseball stadium. "Where the Hanshin Tigers have their games."

"And the national high school baseball tournament," Junpei chimes in.

So many buildings crammed together! So many people! So many cars, all of them shiny and clean and without dents. Osaka bleeds into Kobe, without any break in between.

"Isn't this where that big earthquake was?" I ask.

"Yes," Mariko says. "We felt it even in Tokushima. Over five thousand people died that day."

"It was very early in the morning," my father adds. "We were jolted from our sleep. Okaasan was so surprised that she stood up on the bed."

"Okaasan" means "mother." It takes me a moment to figure out that he's not talking about his mother, my grandmother, but Mariko.

I look out the window, expecting to see cracks in the earth or a broken-down building, but of course it's been almost twenty years since the quake. There is no sign of disaster here.

In Michigan there are tornadoes that uproot trees and peel the roofs off of houses. There are occasionally snowstorms that block the roads and bury cars in deep fluff, and heavy winds, but the earth stays still. Mom has warned me about earthquakes. Even though it's unlikely that there will be another any time soon like the one that struck Kobe, or the one that hit Northeastern Japan three months ago, causing a giant tsunami, I will probably feel smaller quakes, she said. They happen all the time here, on the fault lines.

We leave the city and cross an enormous bridge to another island—"Awajishima," my father says. "The epicenter of the earthquake was here."

I see a Ferris wheel turning up ahead. I wonder if that was here back then. I'd hate to be swaying at the top during a tremor. Just the thought of it makes me shudder.

"Anyone need to use the bathroom?" my father asks, first in English, then in Japanese.

"*Donatsu ga hoshii,*" Junpei says. Then, turning to me, "Mr. Donut."

I nod, pretending to understand.

In any case, we pull into the rest stop, which my father calls a "parking area," and all of us get out of the car. It's not like an American rest stop, where there's a kiosk with tourist brochures, a vending machine, and some toilets. No, this is more like a strip mall. In addition to the Ferris wheel, there is a row of souvenir shops, a cluster of tables with people slurping noodles, a Starbucks, and a place called Mr. Donuts. Ah.

While Mariko and Junpei are standing in line for donuts, I browse in the shops. Stacks of boxes containing individually wrapped cakes cover one long table. Onion cakes! Sweet potato cakes! I see gift boxes of small round green fruit with pocked skin. It looks like some kind of citrus fruit. Another vendor is selling dried seaweed and some kind of snack food made of squid.

I can't help but think of Raoul. He's the most adventurous eater I've ever met, and he's never cooked a dish that I didn't like. For better or worse, I've gained five pounds since he came into our lives. I wonder what he'd make of all of this unusual food. I take my phone out of my pocket and snap a couple of photos to send later.

Back in the car, my father hands me a can of something called Pocari Sweat. Junpei opens the box of donuts and invites me to choose one. I pick a green-tinged donut half coated with chocolate.

"It's matcha flavored," Junpei says. "Japanese green tea."

I take a bite—yum!—then wash it down with a

gulp of Pocari Sweat, which turns out to be a sports drink.

The island of Awaji is nothing like the city we've just come from. Instead of tall buildings and elevated highways there are small farmhouses and onion patches—not much that would topple. Only a few people died here during the Great Hanshin Earthquake. Only a few houses were destroyed.

A dark cloud hangs over the island as if to remind us of that sad day. Soon, raindrops begin to spatter the windshield.

"Now it is *tsuyu*," my father says. "The rainy season. And then it will be very hot."

I lean my head against the window and find myself drifting off to sleep. Every once in a while my head jerks, waking me up. When I see the sign for Aizumi, I perk up. We're almost there! My father takes us off the highway and drives down some narrow back roads past rice paddies and a store called Book Off and greenhouses—"Carrots," he says—and fields of huge leafy plants, which he tells me are lotus roots and corn. They're tiny in comparison to the endless cornfields of Michigan, but the houses are far from the so-called rabbit hutches I read about back in America. There is a series of compounds—palatial mansions surrounded by stuccoed walls. The house at which we finally arrive is one of the more modest ones in the neighborhood, but it's still bigger than I expected.

"Home sweet home," my father says, throwing a glance over his shoulder.

"It looks nice," I say. "It looks . . . new." The roof is the traditional Japanese kind with curved tiles and fish-like creatures leaping from the corners, but I can make out solar panels on top.

"Yes, we rebuilt a few years ago," he says. "But this land has been in my family for two hundred years."

"Wow." As I get out of the car, I notice that there's a tomblike stone structure at the edge of the property. I wonder if my ancestors are interred there. Weird. And a little creepy.

Once again, Junpei grabs my suitcase and leads the way. "*Tadaima!*" he says, sliding the door open.

Mariko bustles into the entryway and sets out a pair of slippers for me. She takes off her loafers and gestures for me to do the same.

I undo the Velcro straps on my shoes, yank them off, and line them up like the other shoes already there. Then I step up, steadying myself with my good hand against the wall, and do my best to slide my feet into the slippers.

"I'll give you a tour," she says.

First, we go into a large Western-style room with a moss-green leather sofa and chairs. A wide-screen TV takes up most of one wall. Along another wall, there are shelves of books in Japanese and a length of indigo-dyed cloth.

"I'll show you the family shrine," Mariko says.

My slippers keep falling off as we shuffle to the back of the house, where there's a room with tatami mat floors and a big black lacquer altar. Above the altar, there is a framed black-and-white photo of a man who I think must be my grandfather, and another one in color of a little girl. She looks to be about three or four years old. She's wearing a red kimono. Obviously, the portrait was taken in a studio on a special occasion. Who is she? The photo is too new to be of some ancestor. Could she be a cousin?

An elderly woman kneels on a cushion in front of the altar. The hair on top of her head is sparse. She looks fragile and small, like something I could scoop up with my one good arm. At first, she doesn't seem to notice we are there.

"This is Obaachan," Mariko says from behind me.

"*Konichiwa*," I say.

She turns her head slightly, but she doesn't speak. I wonder if she is praying. Maybe we have interrupted a private moment and that's why she doesn't bother to greet me.

I glance back at Mariko. Her shoulders rise and fall.

"Who are those people in the photos?" I whisper.

"Ojiisan," she says, pointing to the photo of the

man. Grandfather. "Imoto," she says, pointing to the little girl.

What? I'm too stunned to respond. I must have misunderstood.

But no. My father has come down the hall to join us. He is standing in the doorway. When I look back at him for confirmation, he nods. "Her name was Kana. She was your sister."

5

My sister? I guess I should be used to these crazy, out-of-the-blue pronouncements by now. I found out about Junpei, my brother, in much the same way. After nearly fifteen years of believing that I had no siblings whatsoever, Mom told me in Paris, of all places, that I had this younger brother. She also finally got around to telling me that, contrary to what I'd been led to believe, my father had known about me all along. I wasn't some accidental baby that showed herself after they'd already split up. I can't help wondering what other big surprises the adults in my life have lined up for me. Next time, I'm hoping for something overwhelmingly positive, like *Surprise! You're really a princess!* Or *Surprise! You're bound for wizard school!*

"What happened to her?" I ask my father now.

"She died of leukemia five years ago. She was only four years old."

"Wow," is about all I can say. "That's tough."

I feel a mixture of shock and annoyance. They could have mentioned her sooner. They could have prepared me for this moment.

Obaachan is done with her praying now. When she finally turns, she glares at me.

"Come on," my father says. "I'll show you to your room."

My room smells of fresh tatami mats. There are six on the floor, making this a "six-mat" room. A futon is already laid out on the floor, under a canopy of mosquito netting. There's a lamp with a round white paper shade hanging from the center of the ceiling. My father shows me the cupboard where I'm supposed to stow my futon during the day. A little night-light thing sits in the corner, which he tells me is also for warding off mosquitoes, and a low desk with a cushion for sitting takes up another corner.

The bathroom is down the hall. The toilet is separate, and there are special toilet slippers just for that little room. The toilet itself looks like a spaceship, or something, there are so many dials and buttons. The bathtub is deep. It's also orange, which is a bit unusual. There is a tiled shower area next to it, where I'm supposed to scrub myself before getting into the water. Everyone will use the same water, my father says.

After he's shown me around, he invites me to relax and settle in. "Dinner will be at six," he says. "You can rest until then."

I want to crawl into the netting and collapse on the futon, but I know that I should stay up for as long as I can. Otherwise, I'll wake up the middle of the night jet-lagged and totally off schedule.

I send Mom a quick e-mail on my phone, telling her I've arrived safely. It's the middle of the night in Michigan—too late to call. At any rate, we agreed that we would only talk once a week at most.

"I think it'd be best if you try to immerse yourself," Mom had said. "You'll learn the language faster." And maybe I'll find my place in this family faster, I thought. And my place in Japan.

Dinner is hamburger patties and salad, with bowls of white rice on the side. I notice that there is a fork and a spoon at my place. Everyone else has chopsticks.

"Um, can I have *o-hashi*?" I ask. I don't mean to be ungrateful, but I want them to know that I can use chopsticks, too. They don't have to treat me special.

"Oh! Of course!" Mariko springs to action and comes back with a pair of black lacquered chopsticks painted with tiny rabbits. Everyone else just goes on eating, as if they hadn't heard.

Every now and then I catch Obaachan checking

me out. When I take up the chopsticks, she frowns and says something to my father.

"*Ii wa yo*," he replies in a dismissive tone.

"What?" I ask. "Am I doing it wrong?"

Mariko looks from me to my father and back again.

He sighs. "This is the way that Japanese hold them," he says, demonstrating his grip. His middle finger rests on the lower chopstick, whereas mine had been touching the upper one. "You are a foreigner, so it's okay to eat like that. However you feel comfortable, *dozo*."

I bite back the words that pop into my head. What I want to say is "Yeah, well maybe I'm from abroad, but I have Japanese blood, too." If he had married my mother, I'd even be a Japanese citizen with a passport and everything. I'd be in line to inherit this farm. But I know that's not what he means. He's trying to be polite, to make me feel at ease. I adjust my grip anyway, and it is actually easier that way to pick up clumps of rice.

"You are lucky that you can eat hamburgers all the time," Junpei says. His plate is already clean.

"Well, we don't really." Raoul is our main cook at home, and he's never cooked hamburgers. He's more likely to serve up a Mideastern tagine, or a Mediterranean fish stew. "At my house, we almost never eat this."

"Are you vegetarian?" Mariko asks, suddenly concerned.

"No," I say quickly, not wanting her to think I am rude. She's obviously gone to a lot of trouble to make something that she thought I would like. "I actually love hamburgers. This is delicious!"

With everyone watching me so carefully, I feel obligated to eat everything, even though it's too much, and my stomach is roiling with nerves.

For dessert, Mariko slices pears behind the counter and brings them back on a plate, with toothpicks jabbed into them. Even though I'm stuffed, I try one. Its taste is delicate and sweet, like cologne.

After dinner, I begin to stack the plates, thinking that I will help to clear the table, but Mariko shoos me away. "You must be tired," she says. "Please relax."

Junpei disappears into the house, and Otosan and Obaachan move into the living room area and settle in front of the TV. I follow them, taking my place on a cushion in the corner of the room. I glance at the TV screen and see scenes of destruction—people wandering among piles of debris as tall as this house, people standing in line with jerry cans, waiting for water.

Otosan sighs and shakes his head. "So many people living in shelters," he says.

"Why don't they come here?" I ask. There is plenty of room in this house for another person, or even another family.

"Most of them don't want to leave their homes," he says.

I don't understand. Their homes have been destroyed.

Otosan grabs the remote control and pushes a button. Suddenly, instead of fluent Japanese, a voice-over in British English comes through the speakers.

"This program is bilingual," my father announces.

There is a story about a boy with autism who lost his home in the tsunami. He is living with his family in a school, which has been converted into a shelter. His parents worry that he doesn't understand the magnitude of what has happened—the friends and relatives lost to sea, the destruction of their house and possessions. The boy sits down on a bench in front of a piano. His fingers race over the keys, filling the shelter with ragtime music.

"We think he is playing to comfort himself," the mother says.

An elderly woman manages a smile for the camera. "His music helps us to forget our tragedy," she says.

There's another shot of the boy playing, his body rocking in rhythm with the music, and then the news moves on to something else.

I watch for as long as I can, but the words wash over me, and the images start to blur. I cover a yawn with my hand.

"Why don't you take a bath and go to bed?" Otosan says.

The sun has not yet set, but I nod and leave the room.

6

I wake to the sound of a baby crying. At first, I think it's Esme, but then I remember where I am. I grab my phone and check the time—two p.m. in Michigan, which means it's four a.m. here in Japan.

I slide the paper screen open and look into the dark garden. The baby's cries seem to be coming from next door. A flicker of light comes through the branches. I imagine a mother shifting from foot to foot with the baby in her arms, shushing, like Mom with Esme. The baby becomes silent. I try to go back to sleep, but I can't.

The sun starts to come up about an hour later. I give up on sleep and push back my futon. The house is silent. My American grandparents get up really early, but Obaachan, on the other side of the wall, isn't stirring. I get dressed as quietly as I can, then go down the hall and out the door. I figure I'll have a quick look around the neighborhood before everyone wakes up.

As it turns out, I'm not the first one up. A guy next door is already outside, revving up his tractor. He nods to me as I walk by, suddenly self-conscious of my limp.

"Ohayo gozaimasu!" I say, just loud enough for him to hear. I wish I'd brought a cane. What if I fall in front of this stranger? It happens, and it's always awkward.

I pass the local shrine, which is guarded by concrete creatures that look half lion, half dog. There's a red gate at the entrance. Huge trees tower over the wooden building that is supposedly home to a spirit.

A few houses down, I see a tall figure on a packed dirt lot. It's a guy in a white T-shirt and gray sweatpants. At first, he is completely still, posed like an egret, with one leg bent. I pause, not wanting to interrupt his concentration. He seems to be engaged in some sort of yoga, or maybe it's tai chi. Then he suddenly hurls himself into the air, his arms crossed against his chest, and spins, landing on one foot.

I've never seen anyone move like that before. For a moment, I consider clapping, but he doesn't know that I'm there, that I've been watching. It's too early for strangers to be creeping around, anyway. I back away slowly, carefully, and return to my father's house.

Back inside, I settle on a cushion at the low table

in the living room and write in my journal and sketch until I hear feet on the stairs. Mariko appears, already dressed and made up.

"Did you sleep well?" she asks.

To tell the truth, the pillow packed with buckwheat was kind of hard, and my neck is a little stiff, but I don't want to come across as rude. "Fine," I chirp. "I'm a little jet-lagged, is all."

She ties on an apron and takes a head of lettuce out of the refrigerator.

"Can I help?" I gesture toward the table with my good hand. Maybe I could lay out the chopsticks or something.

"No, no. Please relax."

I think that I should insist, but I feel awkward, so I do nothing as she makes tea and coffee and toast.

Today is Saturday. Junpei doesn't have school, but he gets up in time for breakfast anyway. Soon, we are all at the table with our salads and slices of ham and thick toasted white bread—with the exception of Obaasan. Mariko has prepared a bowl of rice, a piece of fish, and soup especially for her.

"Is this what you usually eat?" I ask, trying to sound casual.

"This is like the breakfast special at a coffee shop," Junpei says. He has already devoured his toast. "It's like American breakfast, right?"

"Um, yeah. Except for the salad."

"What do you have at home?" Mariko asks, now looking worried.

"Different things," I say quickly. "But I don't expect you to feed me like I'm in America. I want to know how you really live. I want to eat Japanese-style breakfast."

My father grunts in approval. His salad is untouched. I'm guessing he's not used to salad in the morning either.

Obaasan slurps her soup loudly, totally oblivious to our conversation. *"Usui,"* she says sharply. Her words are directed at Mariko, who lowers her eyes and murmurs an apology. I guess Obaachan is unhappy with the flavor of the soup. She hasn't looked at me once. After she finishes, she gathers up her array of small dishes, puts them in the sink, and scoops rice into a clean bowl. She pours a cup of tea, puts the tea and rice on a tray, and shuffles toward the back of the house.

My eyes follow her out of the room. *Where is she going with that?*

Mariko reads the question in my eyes. "It's for Kana-chan," she says.

"Oh." For my sister.

After breakfast, Mariko says, "I'll introduce you to the neighbors."

The clock says seven a.m. It seems a little early in

the morning to go visiting but thinking of the guy I saw on the tractor, it occurs to me that seven is late for farmers. "Okay. Um, what should I say?"

"You don't have to say anything," she assures me. "Just bow."

For a second I think that the whole family will go with me, but Obaasan is still in the back of the house, and my father has just opened the newspaper. Junpei dashes upstairs. I guess it's just the two of us.

Mom made me bring a stash of souvenirs—mostly jars of blueberry jam and Mackinac Island fudge—to hand out to people that I meet. I guess this is as good a time as any to distribute gifts. I dig the jam jars out of my suitcase, put them in a tote bag, and hurry to join Mariko, who's waiting in the entryway.

At the first house we go to, the one to the left, a dog starts yapping as soon as Mariko presses the doorbell. We wait for a few beats until an elderly woman with her white hair in a tight bun answers the door. When she smiles, her face crinkles like a dried apple.

Mariko gestures to me. I catch a few words in Japanese: *This is Aiko . . . America . . . summer.*

The woman bobs her head, apparently oblivious to the frantic barking of her fat little Pomeranian.

I hold out a jar of jam and manage to say an all-purpose phrase I remember from my Japanese lessons, *"Yoroshiku onegai shimasu."* It means something like "please," and "from here on out, I'd appreciate your help," and probably some other things, too.

At the next house, a young woman with auburn hair and heavily mascaraed eyelashes comes to greet us. She's carrying a baby on her hip. The baby can't be more than two, but she has tiny gold hoops through her earlobes.

"Hello. You must be Aiko."

The neighbors were obviously prepped for my visit. I wonder what they were told. Do they know anything about my mother? My limp? My Skype chats with Junpei?

"You speak English, too," I can't help blurting out.

"This is Good," Mariko says. "She's from Thailand."

"Yes, we speak English in my country," Good says. "We study at school."

The baby steals a peek at me before hiding her face in her mother's neck. This must be who I heard crying early in the morning. Seeing her makes me miss my little sister.

"This is Chika." Good tries to nudge her face toward me, but Chika resists and whimpers. "She is shy."

"It's okay," I say. "I'm shy sometimes, too." I give her my jam gift.

"If you need any help, come over here," Good says. "Or come play with Chika."

"Thanks. Maybe I will."

We hit up a couple more houses where the wives only speak Japanese, and no one else seems to be around. I wonder if we'll go to the house of that ninja boy I saw this morning, but Mariko heads us back home.

"So what's the story with Good?" I ask. "I thought marriages between Japanese and foreigners are rare."

Mariko nods. "They are, but a lot of young Japanese women don't want to marry farmers. There was a matchmaking party with women from Southeast Asia who wanted to marry Japanese men at the town hall. That's where Good met her husband."

"Huh." Mom told me that my father's parents had been against their marriage because she was a foreigner, but I guess there was more to it than that.

"But you were different, right?" I'm glad Mariko is so easy to talk to. I feel like I can ask her almost anything.

"I grew up on a farm, too," she says. "I like living in the country."

"Did you ever live anywhere else?"

She nods. "I went to Oregon for foreign study when I was in high school. And I studied foreign languages at college in Kobe."

That explains her English. But I wonder why she didn't try to get a job in a big international company or maybe as a tour guide or a teacher.

"Didn't you think you might want to use your English somehow?"

She looks surprised. "But I do. I'm talking to you."

Okay, she's got a point.

"What was my grandfather like?" I ask.

Mariko twists her mouth and looks up at the ceiling. She finally settles on "quiet."

I imagine a henpecked old man trying to stay out of Obaasan's way. She must have been even more formidable when she was young and spry. Maybe he wished that he'd chosen a more docile bride.

"Were they in love?"

Mariko shrugs. "It was an arranged marriage. Your grandmother was the oldest child. She didn't have any brothers. Your grandfather was adopted into the family as the eldest son and heir. He had to change his name."

How extreme! But I guess that explains why Obaasan is so devoted to keeping the farm going. It's her legacy.

"I think they respected each other," Mariko says. "We Japanese don't talk about love so much."

I take her words as a warning: Don't ask her if she loves my father, or if he loves her back. It's none of my business. But I can't help wondering. Did they settle for each other? Has Mariko ever been in love at all? Maybe there was someone in Portland, some totally inappropriate grunge rocker that she was crazy about and wanted to marry, but her parents said no. And what if there wasn't? How sad would that be, to never feel that head-spinning, heart-speeding phenomenon of falling in love?

I know that Mom fell in love with my father. They met in Paris, that most romantic of cities, and she followed him back to Shikoku. But true love doesn't necessarily conquer all. In spite of their love for each other, in spite of me, the child they conceived together, the obligations of land and family had a stronger pull on my father.

I don't really get it. Americans move around all the time. When Mom and I moved out of the little bungalow where we'd lived for over a decade, I felt a little sad, but change is inevitable. I gathered up my memories of playing in the sprinkler on the sloped lawn, and of finding a robin's nest in the juniper tree just outside my bedroom window, and of planting marigolds in the flowerbed alongside the house, and I carried them with me. Now we live in a new house with Raoul and Esme. Someday, we might all move away, and that's fine with me.

Our house in Michigan is virtually plastered with images of Mom, Raoul, Esme, and me. Besides wedding and school photos and framed snapshots from our trip to Paris, Mom's paintings of us hang on the walls. In her studio there are sculptures of me at various ages in different poses. The lack of photos in this house is a little surprising. Other than the portraits above the family altar, no family photos are displayed.

I'm about to ask about this when Mariko opens a cupboard and pulls out a stack of albums. "Would you like to look at these?" she asks.

"Yes!"

We settle down on cushions around the low table in the living room and start leafing through. The first album is full of pictures of my father's and Mariko's wedding. I can't help thinking that while Mariko was getting trussed up in this lavishly embroidered red kimono, Mom was struggling to pay the bills and trying to teach me how to use a spoon. In the photos, Mariko is wearing an ornate wig studded with hair ornaments. Her face is powdered white. She looks like one of those Japanese dolls in glass cases that are only put out on display for Girls' Day. My father is wearing a Japanese outfit, too—black culotte-type pants and a short kimono on top, which are called *hakama*. Meanwhile, my mom would have been wearing a paint-smudged shirt and faded jeans, her hair done up in a messy ponytail. For a second, I wonder what my mother would have worn if she'd married him. Surely not a kimono. I've heard her complain about how tight and restrictive they are, how they keep women from being free.

In another photo, Mariko is wearing a white kimono with a hood. In yet another, she's wearing a Western-style bridal gown, and later the wig is gone, and she's all decked out in a sparkly evening gown with a tiara on her head.

"That's so pretty," I say. "So you wore all of these different dresses on the same day?"

"Yes," Mariko's face takes on a glow as if she's caught up in the memory. "It was like a fashion show."

Apparently the wedding was followed by a big banquet. Some of the photos show the happy couple lighting candles at the various tables full of guests or sitting at a long table covered by a white cloth, a gilded folding screen behind them.

Mom and Raoul had their wedding in our backyard. Mom wore a burgundy sheath. She said she was too old for a frothy white gown.

I grab another album and flip it open. This one is full of photos taken several years later. A younger Obaasan appears with a baby bundled to her back.

"Junpei?" I guess.

"No, that's Kana." Mariko traces the outline of the photo with her index finger.

A few pages later, Kana is bigger, but still strapped to my grandmother's back. "Was she sick here? Couldn't she walk?" Again I wonder why my disability was such a big deal for her.

Mariko laughs. "No, she was healthy then. Obaachan just liked to carry her around. Your grandmother mostly raised Kana, until she really did get sick. I was working with your father all day."

That explains their intense bond. And since Obaasan no longer does much of the farm work and has no more children to raise, maybe she has nothing to do except sit at the altar and hang out with Kana's ghost.

Mariko is easy to talk to, but there are some things that I can't ask her about. Not yet. But maybe I can ask my brother. That afternoon, I grab a pack of cards from my suitcase and knock on Junpei's door. Time for sibling bonding.

"*Hai?*"

"It's me. Aiko."

I hear the click of the lock, and the door opens. Over his shoulder, I see that his bed is unmade and his desk is covered with textbooks and papers and thick pulpy comics. Posters of Major League Baseball stars and of the robot Gundam are pinned to the far wall. A crumpled pair of jeans lies on the floor.

His room is so different from mine. Besides being super messy, it seems more American somehow. In my room back in Michigan, there is a little pot of indigo on the windowsill and a quilt patched together with antique kimonos on my bed. I've got posters of Japanese manga characters on the walls.

"Were you studying?"

"A little." He looks sheepish, as if I've caught him in a lie.

"Oh, sorry. I thought we could play cards." I hold up the deck. "But if you're busy . . ."

He opens the door wider. "It's okay. I need break."

"*A* break," I correct. I've been giving him English lessons via webcam for the past year. He's made a lot of progress. I can't stop now.

Junpei clears a space on the carpet and we plop down on the floor.

"So what card games do you know?"

He names some I've never heard of, or maybe they're just different in English. Hand-wise, Concentration is the easiest for me. I make an executive decision and start laying out the cards facedown in a grid.

He seems to know this game. After a couple of turns, when we're both more relaxed, I ask him about Kana. "What was she like?"

He pauses, searching for words. "She was so cute."

Yes, she was. I saw the photo on the altar: those dimpled cheeks, the straight bangs over big brown eyes, the mouth like a rosebud.

"She loved Miffy."

"Miffy?"

He grabs a pencil and draws something. It's a simple rabbit with no mouth. "Famous character," he says.

"What did she like to eat?"

He flips over a couple of cards—a jack and a ten of clubs—then turns them back over. He thinks for a moment. "She likes curry and rice. And strawberries."

Thinking of Obaasan and her tray of food, I don't correct his tense. Maybe Kana still does like curry and rice, even though she is dead.

"I bet you miss her a lot."

"Yes," he says, and he scoops up a pair of queens.

I finally get a pair myself—two eights, and then, lucky me, two aces.

"*Sugei!*" Junpei looks impressed.

"Why didn't your parents have more children?" I'm not sure that he knows this question, or if he will be able to answer, but I ask anyway.

He shrugs. "They wanted. But no."

"They wanted another baby, but it didn't happen?"

He nods.

Poor Junpei. He's the only one left to carry on the family name, the only one to keep the farm going. Will he be able to find a nice, hardworking Japanese girl to marry him, or will he have to try to find a Thai bride at a party? I can hardly believe that in a country with robots and high-speed trains that people still use matchmakers. It seems like something out of an old-timey novel.

"So now there's just you," I say.

He studies me for a moment. I'm not sure he's understood me, but he finally says, "And you."

That evening, I Skype Mom.

She's obviously just woken up. Her hair is loose, and she's not wearing any makeup. I can see the collar of her favorite plaid pajamas. Every couple of seconds, Esme's hand floats onto the screen. She makes birdie noises.

"Mom . . ."

"Yes, sweetie?"

"Did you know about my sister?" She knew about Junpei way before I did, so why not?

"Of course," Mom says. She leans down, showing me her scalp, her crooked part, and I hear her blow a raspberry on Esme's belly. "I knew the exact moment she was conceived. It was the night of a thunder-storm . . ."

"Whoa, there. I think you're about to reveal too much information," I cut in.

In reply, Mom holds Esme up to the camera. "Look! There's your big sister! Say 'hi' to Aiko!"

Just seeing her moon face makes me feel ten times more homesick. We play peekaboo for a few seconds and then I crawl my fingers toward the camera like I'm going to tickle her through the screen. She watches with total fascination. Then she burps, and a bit of regurgitated milk spews out of her mouth, onto the keyboard.

"Oops!"

I give Mom a second to wipe up the mess and settle Esme on her shoulder. "You were saying?"

"I wanted to know if you knew that I had a sister in Japan."

Now she looks confused. "A sister in Japan?"

"As it turns out, my father and his wife had a little girl who died."

She gasps, as if she's been gut-punched. Immediately, her eyes fill with tears. "I had no idea. Your poor father! And Mariko!"

"They told me about her my first night here. It was kind of weird. Do you think they invited me here because they want, I don't know, a replacement?"

Mom is silent for a long moment. At first, I think it's because I've rendered her speechless. But when she finally does speak again, her voice is all wavery, as if she's trying not to cry. I realize that she's trying to compose herself. "Honey," she says, "Everyone knows that a lost child cannot be replaced."

7

Mom said that if I want to be treated like a member of the family I will have to stop behaving like a guest. On Monday morning, I roll out of the futon, nudge it into thirds, and shove it against the wall. The light duvet that I'd covered myself with goes on top, followed by the buckwheat pillow. After I've dressed and washed my face, I join Obaasan on the verandah where she's already preparing to hang a basket of washed clothes to dry in the sun.

"*Tetsudaimasu,*" I tell her. I will help.

She looks me up and down, as if I'm not taller than she is, grunts, and moves aside. "*Dozo.*"

The laundry goes on a long pole resting on overhanging hooks at each end. With my good hand, I bring the pole down and lean it against my body. I string a couple of pant legs onto the pole and manage to set it back onto the hooks without letting the clean clothes touch the ground.

My grandmother's eyes are on me as I sling towels over the pole and straighten them out before securing them with clips. She doesn't make a move or utter a word until I pin up a T-shirt, then it's *"Dame, dame! Kita no ho wa dame yo!"*

Hmmm. "Dame" means "no" or "forbidden." "Kita" means "north." I remember reading somewhere that the Japanese believe that the Land of the Dead is in the north, and you're not supposed to sleep with your head in that direction. There must be some laundry-related superstition.

I take the shirt down and raise my eyebrows at her. "How should I do it, then?"

She huffs a sigh, snatches away the shirt, and slides it onto one of the plastic hangers kept in a plastic crate next to the washing machine. When the hanger is hooked on the pole, the shirt is no longer facing north, but east, the better to receive the rays of the sun.

I do the same with the next three shirts, but then I accidentally drop one of Mariko's skirts onto the verandah floor. Obaasan starts up with a long stream of syllables. It sounds like she's swearing at me.

"Gomennasai," I apologize, bowing my head.

She tosses the skirt back into the washing machine and points to the door. "You go," she says in English. "Finish."

One little mistake, and suddenly hanging out the laundry is an epic fail. Talk about overreacting. So maybe she is the grandmonster after all.

I pass Mariko as I storm by, my limp suddenly more pronounced than usual, on the way to my room. I should try to help her with breakfast, but I'd probably mess that up somehow, too. There are so many nitpicky rules around here, it's impossible to learn unless you've been brought up with them.

After breakfast, Junpei, looking like a young professional in his starched white shirt, striped necktie, and plaid pants, hops on his bicycle and takes off for school. Summer vacation doesn't begin until the end of July. I'm dreading spending the day in a state of awkwardness with Obaasan when Mariko announces that we will go sightseeing.

Sure, whatever. I will surrender myself to the whole guest/tourist experience. And yes, I do want to see what's around here. Maybe I'll find inspiration for a new episode of *Gadget Girl*. I grab my phone for taking photos and my sketchbook and meet Otosan out at the car. I notice that the grandmonster is nowhere in sight. When I realize that she's not going with us, I relax a bit.

We set out on a whirlwind tour of Tokushima. First we go to Naruto and ride on a glass-bottomed boat to see the giant whirlpools churning up the straits. Then we visit the German House, a museum devoted to German prisoners who were held here during World War I.

Otosan buys the tickets and hands me one. We seem to be the only visitors at the moment. The ticket taker, a middle-aged guy with perfectly pomaded hair, follows us into the room with the exhibits. He seems eager to chat.

"First time to museum?" he asks me in English.

He must have heard me speaking to Otosan and Mariko. How else would he know that I'm not Japanese? I look more Asian than not.

"Yes. First time," I say.

"Very good, very good." He rattles off something in Japanese to my father and his wife while gesturing to a diorama of imprisoned soldiers baking bread. Mariko translates for me. Apparently, the POWs were treated really well. They were allowed to make sausage, had an orchestra, and had events with the locals. Who knew? I've been here for a few days now, and I haven't seen any foreigners other than Good. But at one time, there was virtually a village of Europeans here. *Gadget Girl and the German POWs?*

The museum worker sidles over toward me again, ready to try out some more English. "Exchange student?" he asks.

"Uh, no, actually . . ." I wait for Mariko or Otosan to jump in and say something. *She's our daughter! She was born in Japan!* I know they both understood the question, but neither of them responds. How can I claim them if they won't claim me? "I'm just a tourist," I finally say. I wait for my father to correct me, but he doesn't. Maybe he and Mariko don't want to share details of their private life with this stranger. He doesn't seem like a typical reserved Japanese person. Our guide begins chattering in Japanese again, which I don't understand, but I don't even care what he says. I lag behind, wishing he would go away.

The tour ends and we exit. It's a relief to be outdoors again, away from the images of barbed wire and the sad soldiers' letters to Germany. The quiet after the guide's long-running narration is nice, too. The museum is up against a lushly forested mountain. A sign with a picture of a monkey is stabbed into the side of the hill.

"Cool!" I've never seen a monkey in the wild. I prepare my camera, just in case one pops out of the woods.

Otosan shakes his head. "Not cool. They eat farmers' crops. They mess up TV antenna."

Mariko nods. "The monkeys are so naughty."

"What else is up there?"

Otosan shrugs. "Wild boar, probably. Also, *mamushi* —very dangerous snakes."

Suddenly, the bushes crackled and Gadget Girl found herself face-to-face with a hairy beast. Its pointy tusks were aimed straight at her heart. Meanwhile, a dreaded mamushi coiled at her feet . . .

Okay, I'd rather not run into a snake. Or a wild boar, for that matter. Too much nature may not be such a good thing. I tuck the phone back into my pocket and make my way to the car.

Next, we go to one of the temples that's part of an eighty-eight-temple pilgrimage. A group of pilgrims in white robes and straw hats hovers around the entrance. Most of them carry walking sticks. I perch myself on a bench and make a discreet sketch.

We stop at a noodle restaurant for lunch, then drive to the top of Mt. Bizan—aka Eyebrow Mountain—from which we can see the whole city of Tokushima sprawled out below. Beyond, the Inland Sea sparkles in the afternoon sun. There's another museum at the top of the mountain, this one featuring the relics of a Portuguese sailor who lived at the bottom of the slope in the 1800s. Looking at his portrait, his long white beard, I can't help wondering what the locals made of him. The museum guide tells us that he had a wife and child in Macao, but he later settled in Tokushima and married a young Japanese girl.

"When she died, he married her sister."

Gadget Girl and the Lecherous Sailor? Uh, maybe not.

I'm pretty exhausted by the time we get home. I think that I must have seen all there is to see, but Otosan says, "Tomorrow we'll go have a look at the stone pillars at Dochu. It's like Japanese Grand Canyon."

"Great!" I manage, though all I want to do is crawl into my futon.

Although my body is still pretty much on Michigan time, I force myself to stay awake long enough to watch TV after dinner with the family. Otosan reaches for the remote control.

"You can watch it in Japanese," I tell him. "I'm trying to learn."

He retracts his hand.

Today's disaster feature is about a tomato farmer in Tohoku. He's young, early thirties, with a thin wiry body and sun-browned skin. A photo flashes onto the TV screen—the farmer, smiling, next to a young woman with short hair and three little kids. This is followed by images of a greenhouse full of tomato plants and the family holding baskets of bright red fruit. Next, we see the flooded town, splintered buildings, and piles of rubble. The farmer appears again, in a video, before a household shrine. Photos of his wife and children and an elderly couple, his parents maybe, are arranged on the wall above, like the photos of my sister and grandfather in this house. His name is easy to read—the kanji for mountain and field. I whisper it. "Yamada." The reporter asks him something, and he shakes his head. *"Mo ii."* Which means something like, "I've had enough." Does he mean that he's lost his will to farm? To live? That he's had enough of that place and he wants to relocate? His family and farm are gone. He's young, of course, and he can start again, but maybe he's thinking that his life is over. He has no one to teach, no farm to pass on. What will he do now?

I look over at my father. Is he thinking about his own lost daughter? About how he would feel if he lost his farm? His face is blank. It's hard to tell what's on his mind and hard to ask. Even if I were fluent in Japanese, I can sense that there are a lot of things that we are not supposed to talk about.

"Taihen," I say, trying a new word. It means "very" or "terrible."

He grunts in agreement. *"Taihen, desu ne."*

Almost everywhere we go there's a box on the counter next to the cash register to gather donations for the disaster victims in Tohoku. Every time I see one—at the German House, at the restaurant, at the museum for the Portuguese sailor—I feed a few coins into the slot, but it doesn't feel like enough. I want to do something more to help. Something bigger.

8

After a week of being a tourist, I wake to the smell of rain. It sounds like a waterfall rushing over the roof. When I push back the sliding paper door, I see that the koi pond is nearly overflowing. I remember that it's *tsuyu*. The rainy season.

My first thought is "Yay, no sightseeing today!" I'm a little worn out from rushing from one tourist spot to another. I just want to stay in the house, grandmonster or not, and take it easy for a day or two. While I appreciate his effort, at times it feels as if showing me the sights is my father's way of keeping his distance. If he's out in public narrating the giant whirlpools in the straits of Naruto, we won't have to talk about anything real, anything personal. And those sand pillars of Dochu? They are so not like the Grand Canyon. Mildly interesting, yes. Epic grandeur, no.

I crawl out of my futon and slide the door on the other side open, just an inch or so. Through the crack,

I can see that the futons have been folded and put away in the cupboard. Obaachan is already awake, and probably everyone else is, too.

I pull on a pair of shorts and my T-shirt from the Holland, Michigan, Tulip Festival. By the time I splash some water on my face, bundle my hair into a ponytail (which, thanks to numerous Occupational Therapy sessions, multiple YouTube tutorial viewings, and a lot of practice using my shoulder and the wall, I can now manage in two minutes flat), and get out to the kitchen, Mariko has already laid out a lavish breakfast of grilled fish, soup, rice, and vegetables, each in their own individual dish. At home, we'd just pile everything onto the same plate in order to save on dishwashing.

"*Ohayo gozaimasu*," I say with a bow. It feels ridiculously formal, but this is what we practiced at home. "Be polite," Mom said, over and over, "and you'll get along just fine."

"*Ohayo!*" my father replies. Obaachan ignores me. Junpei is busy shoveling rice into his mouth with his chopsticks, but he nods.

"*Dozo*," Mariko says, motioning to the one empty setting.

I take my place at the table across from my grandmother. Mariko immediately swoops over with a pot of tea and fills my cup.

The fish is laid out on an oblong dish that looks

like it was fired in a kiln. It hasn't been skinned or deboned. It has eyes, which are now blurred from the heat of cooking, but it still feels as if it is staring at me. I feel a sudden craving for Cream of Wheat.

"You eat it like this," my father says. He picks up the halved green globe—some kind of citrus fruit—from the corner of the dish and squeezes it over the length of the fish. "*Sudachi*," he says. "Local special fruit." And then he points to the soy sauce dispenser at the center of the table. "And then add *shoyu*."

Everyone is watching me, so I can hardly slip this fish into my lap for later disposal. I guess I will have to eat it. I take a sip of my tea, stab my chopsticks into the fish and scrape away the skin. Then I pincer some of the white flesh and bring it to my mouth.

Obaachan winces. Okay, so it looks like I'm doing it wrong.

The bones on my father's plate are picked clean. Junpei is still eating, though, so I watch him. He manages to take up chunks of fish, skin and all, and loft them into his mouth. His way of eating is much more elegant than mine. I will have to practice.

The rice is much easier, but I can't hold the bowl well in my left hand, like everyone else does. I set it in front of me and eat with my right hand. Then I pick up my red lacquer soup bowl with one hand and take a sip.

"We've arranged for you to go to school with Junpei," my father says. "Starting tomorrow. I hope that's alright with you."

"Yeah, sure," I say. "I mean, yes." I had mentioned in one of our Skype chats that I wanted to check out Japanese high school.

"Is there a bus stop nearby?" I'm not too good with bicycles, but I can manage public transportation.

They look at me with horror, as if I'd volunteered to forage for my own food or sleep outside.

"No bus," Otosan says. "Mariko will drive you to school." The way he says it, I worry that he might be offended if I refuse.

Mariko nods in agreement and pours more tea into all of our cups.

"Okay," I say, wondering if I will ever be trusted to go anywhere by myself. "Sounds good."

9

When I'd pictured this going-to-school-with-Junpei scenario, I'd imagined shadowing him from class to class. Maybe the homeroom teacher would let me make a brief self-introduction, but mostly I'd stay in the background, out of everybody's way. I certainly didn't imagine *this*.

Junpei and I are sitting in the principal's office on a black leather sofa. The principal, a short guy with a rather obvious comb-over, is leaning forward, examining me as if I were from outer space.

I smile at him. He smiles back, flashing a gold tooth. Junpei is sitting broomstick-straight beside me, his hands curled into fists, which are resting on his knees. It's like he's scared of this guy.

The principal at my high school is a woman. She wears flowered dresses and bold jewelry, and the only time anyone is ever called to her office is when they've won some great honor, like the National Merit Award, or done something truly reprehensible, like puncturing the tires of the teachers' cars or selling ADHD drugs in the girls bathroom.

A woman in a white blouse, navy pencil skirt, and plaid cloth slippers shuffles in with a shiny black tray. She kneels at the principal's elbow and sets a handleless cup of green tea in front of him. The cup is made of pottery, like the fishplates we use at breakfast. Then with the same degree of formality, she sets a cup in front of me and another in front of Junpei.

My throat is parched from nerves. I reach for the tea, but Junpei nudges my leg with his and shakes his head slightly. Only when the principal has taken a loud slurp does Junpei nod at me to do the same.

I can't bring myself to slurp, but I take a little sip.

"*Otani-yaki*," the principal says, pointing to the cup.

I stare back, uncomprehending, waiting for more. Something about the tea—the *ocha*? Its flavor?

The principal gets that I don't understand. He fires off a string of words to Junpei, and gestures to me, then sits back and waits for my poor brother to translate. But it seems that Junpei doesn't have the right words either.

"He says it's . . . uh . . . local . . . uh . . . product." His entire head has turned bright red.

Maybe everyone expects him to be able to speak English because he has family in America. Of course he is embarrassed to let the principal down.

Instead of giving Junpei a break, the principal barks something to the Office Lady who reappears in the doorway, listens impassively, bows, and says *"hai"* a few times. Then she backs out of the room, and he takes another loud slurp and settles back in his black leather chair, looking satisfied.

Nobody speaks. I take a look around. The wood-paneled walls are hung with a series of framed photos of men through the ages. They start out in black and white—men in *hakamas*, which are like kimonos for men, with winged hair and old-timey round spectacles, on to sixty-something men in navy suits and bland neckties. There must be some rule against smiling for photos, or else these were all taken at funerals.

Noticing the direction of my gaze, the principal chuckles and nods. *"Kocho sensei,"* he says, pointing to himself, and then the photos. "Same, same."

Ah, these are portraits of all of the past principals of the school.

"There aren't any women," I say, thinking of Mrs. Hammond at my school back home.

The principal continues to nod and grin. I don't think he understood me, and Junpei doesn't bother to translate my comment. He continues to sit miserably beside me, his hands still clenched into fists.

Just then, the door opens and another male student glides in, out of breath. He's tall and gangly.

I have a flash of déjà vu. Have I seen this guy before? The principal perks up. He instructs Junpei to move to the other side of me, and this new boy to sit beside me.

"This is Watanabe," the man says. "He speak English."

"Hi," the boy says. Even sitting, I have to look up to see his face. "I'm Taiga Watanabe. They asked me to come and translate for you." His accent is of native speaker quality. He sounds like an American. If I closed my eyes, I'd think I was listening to some guy in the halls of my high school.

"Oh." I feel sorry for Junpei again. "Good. I'm Aiko."

The Office Lady brings in another cup of tea and sets it in front of Taiga.

Now that we have someone here who can translate, the principal turns into a veritable chatterbox. He wants to tell me all about this town, this high school, this country. The teacups, he tells me, are made at a local kiln and glazed in a regional style—*Otani-yaki*.

Next, he wants to know about me.

"Where were you born?" Taiga translates.

"Um, *here*."

Everyone looks surprised, including Junpei. Should I go into the story of how my parents met in Paris, how my mother followed my father back here, settled in to learn all about indigo, and then found out she was pregnant? Should I tell them how my grandparents were opposed to their marriage—after all, my mom was a foreigner, an artist, hardly wife material in the eyes of an old-fashioned Japanese farm couple. And then I was born prematurely, and the doctors told my father that I would be disabled, that I might never walk or talk, and my grandmother thought that my mother had brought shame upon the family. I think that would be way too much information. I'll go for the condensed version.

"Yes, I was born in Japan. My mother was studying here, but we moved to Michigan when I was a baby. I don't remember anything about Tokushima."

The principal nods, leans forward, then fires off another question. For better or worse, my story has piqued his interest.

"What do your parents do?" Taiga asks.

"My mom is a sculptor. And my father . . ."

I glance over at Junpei, whose eyes are suddenly filled with panic, as if he doesn't want me to mention our father. It throws me off. *Better not go there.*

"My stepfather is a musician," I say. "And he teaches at college." Raoul does a lot of things. He's also the host of a radio show featuring world music, and he composes, and writes articles for musicology journals. He's a culinary god, as well, but he doesn't get paid for that.

"Stepfather," the principal repeats, nodding, as

if he's mulling this over. *Oh, the Americans and their complicated families. The marriages, and divorces, and remarriages.*

Finally, he drains his cup with a final slurp, and gestures toward the door. "We go? You will give self-introduction to students."

I imagine a classroom full of students. How many will there be? Fifteen? Twenty? And what should I say? I can try out my Japanese. *"Ohayo gozaimasu!"* I rehearse in my head. *"Hajimemashite!" It's nice to meet you!*

Junpei, Taiga, and I trail after the principal as he saunters out of the office, down the corridor, to the gymnasium. When he pushes the door open, I see that the gym is full of students sitting on the floor. It's clearly a school assembly. *For me?* Okay, I'm ready to get out of here now. I glance back at the door, wondering how I could make my exit. Should I say I have cramps? Guys tend not to ask too many questions when a girl alludes to "woman troubles." Should I pretend I'm about to faint? Is there a fire alarm button that I can push? Help! I don't want all of these people looking at me!

"Please," the principal says, gesturing to a row of folding chairs against the wall. "Sit down."

I submit to his orders. Just call me "Aiko the Meek." Taiga takes the seat beside mine, and Junpei sits next to him.

Everybody's focused on the stage, where there's a podium backdropped by the Japanese flag. From my slightly elevated position, I look across the sea of dark heads.

I've seen magazine layouts of the youth of Japan, which always seem to feature hyper-fashionable Harajuku girls with dyed blonde hair and eyelashes as extensive as a daddy longlegs's appendages. Well, we're not in Tokyo anymore, Toto. There is no dyed hair, no makeup or piercings. There are no watches or jewelry—no sign of bling whatsoever—or any other mark of individuality. All of these kids are in uniform—long-sleeved white shirts or blouses paired with pants or skirts in a subtle navy plaid. If we were in Michigan, everyone would be sitting cross-legged, or with their legs comfortably to the side. They'd be relaxed. *Chill.* Here, everyone seems frozen, rigid, like Junpei in the principal's office. Their knees are drawn up in front of them, their hands clasped like belts around their legs.

Another guy, a teacher, apparently, stands up and strides to a microphone stand just to the right of the stage. He bows to the flag, to the principal, and then to the students, who bow back from their seated positions. When he opens his mouth to speak, his voice booms out across the gymnasium.

When he finishes his spiel, a male student climbs

the steps to the stage, bows to the flag, and takes his place behind the podium.

"He's the president of the student council," Taiga whispers. "He's talking about a school project to help the relief effort in Tohoko."

I try to pick up as many words as I can. I catch "newspaper" and "recycle." Apparently, they're having some sort of paper drive to raise money for earthquake and tsunami victims.

After another series of perfectly choreographed bows, the student takes his seat and the teacher acting as master of ceremonies starts to speak again.

I hear my name and Junpei's, and "Amerika" and the word "*itoko*." He seems to be introducing me to the student body. That last word sticks in my head. *Itoko* doesn't mean sister. It doesn't even mean half sister. That guy just introduced me as Junpei's *cousin*.

I lean forward a little and catch Junpei's eye. "*Itoko?*"

He looks uncomfortable. "*Ato de . . .*" he says in a low voice, meaning, I guess, that he will explain later.

Beside me, Taiga raises his eyebrows. "Do you want me to translate?"

"No, it's okay," I say. I think I understood just fine. Someone—my father, or his wife Mariko—must have told the school that I am Junpei's cousin visiting from America because the truth is too complicated

73

or shameful. My parents weren't married. Unwed mothers, bastard children—they must be a big deal here. I don't want anyone to be embarrassed by my presence, but I can't help feeling hurt. Why did my father invite me to visit if he wasn't ready and willing to claim me as his daughter?

I'm so caught up in my thoughts that I miss my cue. When I tune back in to the present, I see that the principal is staring at me expectantly. He's saying, "*Dozo, dozo.*"

Taiga gives me a nudge. "He wants you to introduce yourself. You can speak in English. They can all understand a little."

"On the stage?" My mouth is suddenly a desert. My heart is trying to jump out of my chest. "In front of all of those people? There must be hundreds!"

I take a deep breath and stand, steadying myself with the back of the chair. Don't think about all those people, I tell myself. Think about your feet. I put one foot in front of the other and make my way slowly, slowly to the steps. I can do this. I can do this. I can do this. I plant my right foot on the first step, swing my left foot up, and adjust my balance. Step, swing, steady, repeat. The gymnasium is completely silent. Everyone is watching me. It seems like hours before I reach the stage. A bead of sweat dribbles down my back. When I finally plant my feet on the stage, I exhale in relief. I don't even think about bowing to the flag.

I take another step, and another, and, oh, this can't be happening now, I feel my left leg giving way. My good hand flails out ahead of me as I stumble. *No, no, no.* Titters ripple across the gymnasium followed by a teacher's sharp reprimand. A hush falls again. I grab onto the podium and steady myself. Heat flares on my face. Down below, rows of students stare up at me, their faces blank, expectant. They're waiting for me to speak. I look out at the sea of students and try to imagine them all in their underwear. When that doesn't work, I fill my lungs and then exhale slowly. Breathe in, breathe out. Repeat.

"G-g-good morning." Ugh. Ten minutes ago, I thought I'd impress them with a few words of Japanese, but now I can barely greet them in English. My armpits dampen. "I-I'm, uh, Aiko Cassidy. I, uh, look forward to getting to know you and learning about Japan. Thank you."

I turn away from the podium, back toward the stairs, but I can't seem to move forward. There's no way I can make it back down the stairs. Tears blur my vision.

Suddenly, out of the corner of my eye, I see someone rise and leap up the stairs. My déjà vu kicks in again and my mind clicks: It's the spinning boy! I blink and see Taiga standing in front of me. He holds out his arm like an usher at a wedding. "Shall we?"

I grab onto his arm. From out on the floor, I hear girls' voices rising in disbelief. It sounds like *"Ehhhh?"* My humiliation is complete.

As Taiga guides us forward, down the stairs, and back to our folding chairs, I can feel the heat of his skin, and the tautness of his forearms. I haven't been this close to a boy in maybe a year, not since I rode on the back of Hervé's scooter down the streets of Paris, but I'm too embarrassed to feel anything but shame. Even without a mirror, I know l that my face is strawberry red.

Taiga speaks to me softly under his breath. "Ignore them," he says, when the girls' voices rise up again.

"Just a little bit more," Taiga whispers. "You're almost there."

Finally, I'm back in my seat.

"Are you okay?" Taiga asks.

"Yeah, I think so." I can't even look him in the eye.

I'm only half aware of the close of the assembly. The teacher who'd made the opening remarks returns to the mic and says something in Japanese. The students on the floor stand up and bow in unison. And then, I guess, it's over. Everyone starts herding out of the gymnasium.

The principal says a few words to Junpei, who turns to me. "Come on," he says, averting his eyes. "We go to my classroom now."

I look around for Taiga to say thanks, but he's already disappeared into the crowd.

"Do you know that kid?" I ask Junpei, as I struggle to keep up. "Taiga?" I figure he must, since he lives only a few houses away, but they didn't seem all that friendly.

"He's new here," Junpei says. He pauses for a moment as if searching for the right word. "He's a refugee."

"A what?" I think I must have heard him wrong. That boy doesn't look like he came from some war-torn country. There aren't even any wars going on around here, are there?

"His house was destroyed by the earthquake."

"Oh." I recall images of splintered houses washed away by the tsunami, people huddled in school gymnasiums, villages of tiny prefab houses. I didn't think any of that would touch me here, so far away in Tokushima on the island of Shikoku. Taiga was one of the homeless, but he'd had someplace to escape to, someplace better than a shelter, at least.

I'm suddenly ashamed by my shame. My problems are so trivial compared to his. I wish I could run down the hall and find him (not that I can run). I want to tell him how sorry I am, and maybe give him a hug. But then Junpei grabs my arm and pulls me into a classroom. "This is it," he says. "My homeroom."

I take a deep breath, trying to reset myself. "Wow. So many students!" Five rows of desks eight deep take up most of the room. The windows are open, but there's not much of a breeze. A fly buzzes in the corner. Some girls pat at their perspiring faces with handkerchiefs. A couple of them look over at me, lean their heads together, and say something behind their hands. They don't seem too friendly. I guess there are mean girls everywhere.

The homeroom teacher is model-skinny. She looks to be about thirty years old. Her hair is cut in a sharp bob, and her eyebrows have been plucked into thin arches. "Welcome," she says to me now in heavily accented English. "You can sit next to Junpei."

I take the chair next to Junpei's desk. Some of the students look over at me with curiosity. They study my face, my curled hand, and my non-regulation slippers. I have a sudden urge to crawl under a desk and hide. I worry that I will have to do another self-introduction, but the teacher launches into the lesson.

"Open your English books to page eighty-seven."

The students spend most of the class reading aloud from the textbook and then translating each sentence. I manage to pick up a few new Japanese vocabulary words, but mostly I let my mind wander, thinking about my complicated family, and the earthquake and tsunami that brought Taiga here, and that fly that keeps bumping against the window glass and can't seem to find its way back outside.

10

While the class reads aloud from the textbook and copies new vocabulary words, I take out my sketchbook. As soon as my pencil hits the page, I feel calmer. It's as if I'm entering the picture, flowing into the lines I've made, escaping from the world.

At first, I draw the things in the room—the droopy plant next to the window, the panda charm dangling from a student's pencil case zipper, the back of someone's head. Without even thinking about it, I start to draw Taiga. There's something special about him, beyond his English ability and the way that he spins. He seems almost otherworldly. If only I'd met him under different circumstances.

When I finally rest my pen and look up, I realize that a girl off to my left is staring at my drawing. She catches my eye and sneers before turning to whisper to another girl on the other side of her. My face heats up and I quickly close the notebook.

At the end of English class, the students stand in unison and bow to the teacher. She bows back to them. I stay in my chair, confused by what's going on. I'm thinking that we will have to change classrooms, like we do at my school in Michigan, but the teacher gathers up her books and pens and exits the room. A few students spring out of their seats and into the hallway, but others stay put and start chattering to each other, or put their heads down on their desks for a brief rest until the next lesson. I glance back at those girls. They seem to be talking about me again.

"It's boring, isn't it?" Junpei says to me.

"No," I lie. "Not at all." The chair is uncomfortable, and the room is too hot. I try to tell myself that I am having an authentic Japanese school experience, gossipy girls and all.

Another teacher—a guy with floppy hair and glasses this time—comes in for Social Studies, and another woman teacher who looks close to retirement arrives for a lesson in calligraphy after that.

I watch as Junpei prepares his ink and brushes. He hands me a sheet of paper and a brush.

"Will it come out in the wash?" I ask, eyeing the black liquid and my borrowed white shirt.

Junpei shrugs. "Try not to spill."

The teacher writes a kanji character on the blackboard, and then demonstrates with the brush, each stroke leaving an elegant swipe. It looks like a sideways *W* with three smudges underneath beside a double cross. I don't know what it means, but it's beautiful, like an abstract painting. I watch Junpei and try to copy.

The teacher walks between rows, making comments as she goes. When she gets to us, she murmurs something, then lifts my elbow a bit. She watches as I paint a line down the page. *"Mo ikkai."*

"What?" I look to Junpei for translation.

"She wants you to do it again," he says.

So I guess I did it wrong. Story of my life. I crumple the sheet and prepare another piece of paper, feeling totally wasteful. This time, she guides my arm, when I reach the end of the stroke, she puts a little pressure on my hand. The end of my line looks like a frayed black rope. "Yes!" she says in English.

"What does this character mean, anyway?" I ask Junpei.

He glances up from his own painted word. *"Kizuna.* It's . . ." He puts down his brush and holds his hands tightly together.

"Friendship?" I guess. "Cooperation?"

The girl sitting in front of Junpei has overheard us. She turns around to say, "It means 'bonds of friend-ship.'" Her smile reveals a mouthful of misaligned teeth.

"Oh, nice. Thanks."

"I'm Sora," she says, holding out her hand formally. "'Sora' means 'sky.'"

I reach out with my good hand. "Aiko," I say. "'Indigo child.' Nice to meet you."

We paint the same character over and over, until I finally feel like I'm getting the knack of it. *Kizuna*," I whisper with each stroke of the brush. "Bonds of friendship." I think of Whitney back in Michigan, and wonder if she's going to the beach today. I think of Hervé in Paris, bent over his desk as he translates the latest issue of my manga *Gadget Girl*. I think of the bond that I have with Raoul, which is sort of like friendship, but feels more and more like family. With each swish of the brush, I'm seized by homesickness. Why did I ever think I could fit in here? I may stick out in Michigan, but I don't belong here, either.

Every time I finish a version of the character, Junpei carefully lifts my sheet of paper and lays my work out to dry. Finally, he says that we have to choose the one we think is best to turn in.

"This one," I decide, looking at my final attempt. The slashes of ink are bold and stylized. Not bad, if I do say so myself. I pick up the corner of the paper I've just finished painting. It curls inward, and I try to snap it to straighten it out, but the ink runs and jumps out onto my shirt. Great. Now I've got a huge black comma on my chest, and I bet it's permanent.

"Oops," Junpei says.

Amazingly, he and everyone else have managed to keep clean. "Why don't you wear smocks or old shirts or something?" I ask, feeling grumpy. Even Mom expects to get dirty when she's making art. She would never try to paint or sculpt in a pristine white cotton shirt. She always needs a shower afterwards.

"In elementary school, yes," Junpei says. "But now we are in high school."

"That explains it," I mutter.

Although it seems like a good idea to take off the shirt and soak it in water, I'm afraid that the spot might spread. Also, I don't have a change of clothes, and I don't want to go around with a wet splotch on my chest for the rest of the day. I have no choice but to wear it as is, like a mark of incompetence and shame.

When the school day is finally over, Mariko comes to pick me up in the truck. She takes one look at my face and another at my ink-spattered blouse and says, "You must be tired." Thankfully, she doesn't press for more.

As soon as we are back at the house, I change my clothes and hand over the blouse for laundering. Then I flop onto my futon and take a nap until dinner.

Mom and I have agreed to Skype at nine p.m., which is seven in the morning over there, but I can't wait that long. I take a chance and dial her up an hour earlier, hoping she'll be online.

The electronic melody coming from my computer is soothing. My tension ratchets down a notch or two. I feel even better when Mom's face appears on the screen. Her hair is disheveled and she's wearing pajamas.

"Hi, honey. Did you forget the time difference?" She hides a yawn behind her hand. I obviously woke her up. And who knows how much sleep she got last night with a baby in the house? I'm a bad daughter for disturbing her slumber.

"I'm sorry," I say. "I just wanted to talk to you." And then I burst into tears.

Immediately, she's wide awake. "Oh, honey. What happened?"

So I tell her all about my grandmonster's behavior and the horrible school assembly and how I was introduced as Junpei's cousin.

"Oh, Aiko . . ." Tears glisten in her eyes. As if on cue, Esme starts squalling in the background, but Mom doesn't budge. She stays right there with me, even though her instincts are probably telling her to scoop up that baby.

"I want to come home," I say, while I've still got her attention. At this moment, I've never wanted anything more in my life. I want a real-life, real-time hug from my mother. And then I want to snuggle under my kimono patchwork quilt and stare at my Ghibli posters and listen to Raoul on the radio. And then I want to go over to Whitney's house for a black-and-white movie marathon and bowls of popcorn and hours of girl talk about shopping and boys and our futures. And then I want to roll around the floor with my baby sister and blow raspberries on her stomach and feel her pull my hair. I don't want to be with the grandmother who can't stand the sight of me and the father who won't claim me as his daughter and the gorgeous boy who saw me stumble and my ghost of a sister. "Can you call the airline and change my reservation?"

"Are you sure? You've only been there for a few days. Maybe you should give it a little more time."

Esme's crying is getting louder and louder. It occurs to me that Mom doesn't want me to come home. She has enough to deal with as it is. As a struggling single mother and my sole guardian, she's always had too much to deal with. Except for the occasional overnight stay at my Michigan grandparents' house, this is the first time in her life that she's had a break from me. For once, she can enjoy being the normal mother of a normal child with a husband. She is experiencing a full family life for the first time ever. Even so, I want to go home.

Mom peers steadily into the camera, but I can feel

her attention wavering. I have only seconds to make my case.

"Whatever happened to 'If you want to come home early, just call?'" I ask. My voice is whiney, petulant. I hate the way I sound, but I can't help myself.

Her eyes flick to the side, then back at me. I can tell that she's torn between her angst-ridden teenaged daughter and her mini-me. To her credit, she stays put.

"Look," she says firmly. "I know you're disappointed, and I know it's not easy. But you've been wanting to go to Japan and spend time with your father for the past ten years. If you leave now, you may never have another chance to get to know him."

We stare at each other for a moment, as if each of us is waiting for the other to give in. Esme cries. "Wah! Waaaah!" I'm thinking Plan B: Run away to Tokyo. Maybe things are better there. A big city is bound to be more cosmopolitan. I wouldn't stand out so much in a place where there are other foreigners. Or Plan C: Stow away on a plane to Paris. The Parisians know me as my artist mother's muse. She was in a magazine there. The French would welcome me. Maybe I could hang out with Hervé and his family.

"Maybe you'd better go take care of Esme," I say. "You know you want to." My voice is snippy, but I don't care.

Finally, Mom sighs. "Why don't you give it one more week? If you still feel the same next Friday, I'll change your ticket and you can come back home."

Okay. That's better. "Thank you," I say. Guilt instantly kicks in.

"I love you, Aiko."

"Love you, too."

We sign off. I should be relieved, but I feel more like a failure. Or a spoiled brat. She's right. I've pestered her for practically all of my life for this chance to come to Japan, but nothing has turned out the way I expected.

A little while later, there's a knock at the door.

"Aiko-chan?" It's Mariko.

"Yes?" I look around for something to pull over my head. Without even looking I can tell that my face is blotchy from crying. I don't want her to see me like this, but it can't be helped. The door slides open, and there she is.

She kneels beside me. "I heard that you had a bad day." Junpei must have told her what happened. Or maybe the school called.

"Yeah, it wasn't so great."

She hesitates for a moment. "Do you want to stay here tomorrow?"

Tears of gratitude well up in my eyes. I nod. I never want to go back to that school or see those kids again, even if it means being stuck here alone with the grandmonster.

"Okay. I'll call the school and tell them that you won't be going back."

She reaches over and squeezes my shoulder. She's being so kind that I can't bring myself to tell her that I want to leave early. Her feelings will be hurt.

"Thank you," I say. "I think I'll feel better in the morning after a good night's sleep."

Because of my nap earlier in the day, I'm awake for half the night. I finally fall asleep and dream about falling on the stage. In the dream, I don't just stumble. I crash to the floor. My skirt flies up exposing my underwear and howls of laughter fill the gymnasium. Even Taiga is bent over, laughing hysterically.

It's a relief to wake up long after everyone else and find myself alone in the house. Mariko has left a note saying that she will be back for lunch. I guess she's helping my father with the indigo. My grandmother is probably tending Kana's grave.

I toast a slice of bread and pour myself a glass of cold barley tea.

According to the clock, it's eight in the evening in Michigan. Maybe Whitney is home. It would be good to talk to her right about now. I dial her up, and sure enough, she appears on my screen.

"I'm coming home in a week!" I tell her. "We

can go to the Coast Guard Festival together!" Every summer there's a carnival and a parade and a bunch of other events in our town. Until now, we've never been able to do them together because Whitney has usually been in California visiting her dad. "We can go to the beach!"

"What?" She seems disappointed. "I thought you were going to get all inspired and write this magnum opus about being in Japan."

Silence.

"Have you even started?"

Whitney is sort of like my manager or agent or cheerleader. Whatever you want to call it. She's always been my number one fan. Before I even started signing my real name to my *Gadget Girl* manga, when I was intent on staying incognito, she helped me hide my secret identity *and* distribute my manga. She's the one who encouraged me to enter the Japan Shojo Manga Contest, which is how one of my illustrations appeared in one of the most popular monthly comic magazines in Japan.

"I've made some preliminary sketches," I tell her, my eyes sliding away from the camera. "I'm still waiting to have an adventure."

"Make something up!" she says. "Isn't that what creativity is all about?"

"I guess." I'd rather not talk about my lack of artistic progress. Or Japan. I opt for deflection. "So how are things with Luke?" This should keep her going for another twenty minutes, I figure.

But no. "We broke up," she says. "End of story."

"Wh-a-at?"

"He met someone at the pool where he's life-guarding who's a little more . . . willing."

I can't believe it. Two weeks ago they were so in love. Or so I thought. I guess you never know what's happening in someone else's relationship. "Well, that sucks. I'm sorry."

"Don't be. I'm pouring all of my heartbreak into *my* creativity. I've made a million new sketches for costumes for next year's musical." She disappears off-screen for a moment. When she comes back, she's wearing a wide-brimmed hat adorned with flowers. Very Kentucky Derby. "Ta-da! I made it myself. We're doing *Hello, Dolly!*"

"Nice. Make me one, too."

"So how's it going over there? Meet any hot guys among the rice paddies?"

"Well . . ." What difference does it make since I'm leaving in a week anyway?

She draws closer to the camera. "I knew it! You did meet someone! Tell!"

"Okay, there's this one guy. He's really cute and he speaks English perfectly."

"And?"

"And nothing. He was called in to interpret for

me. And then he escorted me off the stage." I can't bring myself to tell her about my supreme humiliation. She'd be sympathetic, of course. She's seen me fall at inopportune times, like when I was walking down the school corridor on my way to lunch and some evil boy stepped on my sandwich. But I know that she sees me as this brave adventurer, coming to Japan all by myself, and I don't want to disappoint her. "I touched his arm. Through his shirt."

"Oooh. A summer romance!"

"Yeah, right. I just met him yesterday. He probably has a girlfriend."

"Well, hurry up and find out. You only have a week."

That afternoon, I'm splayed on my futon watching videos on my computer when the doorbell rings. I hear Mariko's brisk steps, the door sliding open, and high-pitched voices. Probably one of the neighbors bringing vegetables from their garden, I think, but Mariko comes to my door.

"Aiko-chan," she says, sticking her head inside the room. "Someone is here to see you."

She waits until I close my laptop and rise to my feet. I follow her into the living room where Junpei's homeroom teacher and Sora, the girl who sits in front of him, are sipping cold tea from tall glasses. As soon as they see me, they jump up and bow.

I bend awkwardly, confused.

"I am teacher," the woman says, "and this is Sora, class leader. She said you have met already."

"Yes." I nod at Sora.

"We are so sorry you had a bad experience at school," the teacher says, her words sounding rehearsed. "We would like you to come back again so that you will be able to return home with a happy memory of Japan."

They came all this way for me? I'm not even a regular student. The teacher probably has papers to grade and lessons to plan. And Sora is probably missing out on hanging out at a coffee shop reading manga with her friends or something. A wave of guilt crashes over me.

"Oh, p-please don't feel bad," I say. "I think I have many happy memories of Japan already." Well, not exactly, but who cares? My misery is not their fault.

Sora reaches over and tugs on my right hand. "You have to come to school tomorrow!" she says. "You have to come to manga club!"

I didn't know there was such a thing. Well, that does sound fun.

I glance over at Mariko, who is standing off to the sidelines, watching me. Hope glimmers in her eyes.

I take a deep breath. "Okay. I'll give it another try."

11

My second day of school goes a little better. There are no speeches on the stage, no wild ink paintings flinging ink on my once-again white shirt. (Luckily, the blotch came out in the wash.) At noon, Sora turns around and says, "Do you want to eat together?"

Junpei averts his eyes. He seems to shrink into himself. Apparently, they are not bonded by friendship, but I have nothing against her. "Sure."

Mariko made bentos for Junpei and me this morning. Mine is tucked in my backpack, which is stowed in Junpei's cubbyhole at the rear of the classroom. Nothing is locked here. Everyone is so trusting, which is kind of amazing.

Junpei offers to get our lunches and skulks away before I can respond.

The girl leans close to whisper. "He's a shy boy."

So that's it, huh? Maybe he has a crush on this girl.

She pushes her desk up against Junpei's so that we can eat together. Sora has brought her lunch, too, packed in a pink Hello Kitty container. She waits until Junpei has presented me with my bento, a more subdued black lacquer box, before lifting the lid. So many colors! There are broccoli flowerets, a cherry tomato, sausages, and a piece of fish. It's just like the beautiful bentos I'm used to seeing on the Internet, except there are no animal shapes or cartoon characters. We're in high school, after all.

I unwrap and open my box: A crisply fried shrimp and a glazed meatball are nestled in shredded cabbage. Flower-shaped carrot slices are tucked into the mix. There's a dollop of potato salad and half of a hard-boiled egg. Everything is arranged just so, like a painting. I can't help comparing this to the sandwiches that my mother used to slap together for my school lunches five minutes before I went out the door. Mariko obviously put a lot of care and thought into this, and I'm not even her real daughter.

"Is it true that American high school students can go to McDonald's for lunch?" Sora asks. "Like in movies?"

I laugh, wondering what other ideas she and her classmates have about life in the United States. "Yeah, I guess. But this is much better."

"So what comes next?" I ask Junpei. My brain is fried from listening to Japanese all day and trying to understand. I just want to put my head down on a desk and have naptime.

"Art," he says.

"Oh! That should be fun."

He scowls. Obviously, he doesn't share my enthusiasm for color and line.

"And after that, club activities." He's already told me that he's in the robotics club. Although I'm not all that interested in making robots myself, it might be cool to see what they're up to. I wonder what other kinds of clubs meet.

Art is held in another room, so I follow Junpei and several of his classmates down the corridor to a wide studio filled with rows of easels. A mannequin dressed in a sailor-collared school uniform stands in one corner. Watercolors of pieces of fruit are pinned along the wall. Although they seem to be the work of different students, they are strikingly similar, as if they've been painted by number.

The art teacher turns out to be a guy with hair down to his shoulders. He wears a white lab coat, like a doctor. The coat should be paint-stained, I think, but it's pristine.

"I will introduce you," Junpei says. He leads me to the teacher and says, "This is my, um, Aiko. She's visiting from America."

"Welcome," the teacher says in English. "I'm Mr. Ueno." He gestures toward the easels. "Please, anywhere."

"Thanks." I follow Junpei to the back and take my place next to him. Sora is on the other side of me.

The bell chimes, signaling the beginning of class. Mr. Ueno issues a greeting, and then the class leader tells everyone to bow. Even art class seems to be conducted with military precision.

I let the teacher's words wash over me. Before me, a blank piece of paper is pinned to the easel. At my right is a box of colored chalk. Mr. Ueno drags the mannequin to the front of the class and adjusts her limbs so she is standing with arms akimbo. I figure out that everyone is supposed to draw her, but I'd rather draw a living, breathing person. I take a long look at my brother and grab a piece of chalk.

I start with the fuzzy head, bent toward the neighboring easel, and then quickly sketch out the curve of his shoulders and back, and the length of his arm. When I've got the basic shape down, I begin to refine, adding shadows and contours. I'm so engrossed in my work that I hardly notice the passage of time or the footsteps of the teacher as he paces between the rows of students, stopping from time to time to offer a comment or suggestion.

When he reaches my chair, he stands behind me, saying nothing. In my Michigan high school, I am the daughter of the renowned sculptor Laina Cassidy. Every art teacher I've ever had has looked at my work with heavy expectations. For once, I'm just an anonymous art student. Mr. Ueno has probably never even heard of my mother. I wait for him to give me some encouragement. I think my work is pretty good. But he remains silent. Maybe he's disappointed that I didn't follow instructions, choosing to do my own thing instead. I glance over at Junpei's easel. He's managed a fairly primitive approximation of the mannequin. He's not super talented, but at least he's sticking to the assignment. Finally, Mr. Ueno grunts and moves on.

By the time the chime rings again, my portrait is more or less finished.

"*Sugei!*" Sora says. "That's Junpei, right? You're really good!"

"Thanks." I steal a look at hers. She's managed to make the mannequin look like a manga character with sparkling saucer eyes. It's not a true likeness, but it's more original. "I like yours, too."

"Ueno sensei won't like it," she whispers. "Not the same."

"Well, you have to find your own style," I tell her.

"In this class, we must copy," she says. "Usually."

I look up and notice that there is an example of a chalk portrait of the mannequin posted at the front of the room. I wonder if the students were supposed to be imitating Mr. Ueno's work.

The class leader calls out *"Kiritsu!"* Once again, all of the students bow in unison, and then they gather up their art supplies and file out of the room.

"See you later," I say to Junpei.

He holds up his hand, waves.

My new friend grabs my right hand, as if I'm a small child. In the hallway, I catch sight of Taiga leaning against a wall, writing something on a piece of paper. He's surrounded by girls. I can hear them making pigeon noises. He finishes with whatever he's scribbling and hands it to one of the girls. What, is he signing autographs? Before I can manage to catch his eye, Sora tugs me off to the room where the manga club is held.

"Konnichiwa!" she says as we step across the threshold.

A dozen or so students, boys and girls, are scattered around the room, already busy with sketchpads and pens. They look up in unison.

"New face," Sora says, gesturing to me.

"Aiko, desu ne?" asks one girl. She must remember me from the assembly. How could she not? Remembering my moment of shame, I wilt a little bit, but this girl motions me into a chair beside her.

When the bell chimes, the female teacher in charge of the club joins us. She seems mildly surprised to find me there, but quickly recovers. She orders everyone to introduce themselves to me.

"I'm Yuma," says one boy with spiky hair. He holds up a drawing of a ninja that looks a lot like Naruto.

"Yukiko *desu*," squeals another girl. She does a little curtsy, then flips her sketchpad open to a female character drawn in all-out rococo attire, like someone who does all her shopping at Baby the Stars Shine Bright.

Then there's Saho, who is drawing a manga story about two boys in love, and Reiko, whose work in progress seems to be about a girl band on another planet, which is pretty cool.

"Do you draw manga, Aiko?" the teacher asks, leaning back against the desk with her legs and arms crossed.

"Um, yeah." I grab a pen, whip open my sketchbook, and quickly draw Gadget Girl, the heroine of my magnum opus.

A low buzz starts up. I've managed to impress them.

"It's so cool!" Yukiko squeals. "You have to go with us on our excursion to UFO Table this Saturday!"

"UFO Table?" I picture a flying saucer and a trip to space.

"Don't you know?" Sora's jaw drops in amazement. "It's an anime studio!"

"Oh! In that case, I'd love to go."

Just like that, I'm one of the gang.

★ ★ ★

That evening the TV news disaster feature shows volunteers in hazmat suits shoveling piles of dead fish and debris.

"Could I—could we—go up there and help?" I ask. I'm not too good with shovels, but there must be something I can do. It doesn't seem right for me to be living it up 24/7 while people are suffering in the north.

Otosan shakes his head. "They won't take any volunteers who are less than eighteen years old."

"Oh." So what can I do? I've already bought a "Save Japan" T-shirt and donated money.

The camera cuts to a scene at a shelter. Some families are still living all crammed together in tiny spaces. A famous soccer player appears, and the kids start shrieking and smiling. The soccer player reaches into a bag, pulls out a ball, and kicks it to one of the kids. A game begins. Just like that, the children forget what they have lost, if only for a little while.

12

I sleep later the next morning. My body clock is slowly adjusting, switching over to Japan time. I open my eyes. There's just enough light for me to make out the shapes of the bushes outside the window. I hold my breath for a moment and listen. Silence. As far as I can tell, everyone else is still asleep, which means I can probably slip into the street without being noticed. This time I grab a notebook with a Sharpie clipped to the cover before heading out. The sound of the lock clicking seems as loud as a gunshot. I flinch and freeze, listen again. Still, nothing. I slide the door open, shut it, and make my way down the road.

What if I'd lived here all along? If Mom had married Otosan, I would have grown up in this house. Maybe I would have played on the swings next to the shrine that I go past or chased butterflies down these streets. Without Mariko and Junpei to remind me of my other family, without Esme, I can almost imagine a parallel universe in which I belong here.

I look ahead, startled to find Taiga coming toward me. He's not twirling and spinning in the yard today, but jogging. My first impulse is to dive behind some bushes and hide, but I remember that I have yet to properly thank him for rescuing me. I stop and wait until he reaches me.

"*Ohayo!*" he says, coming to a halt right next to me.

"Oh, hi!" Ugh. Why didn't I at least brush my hair before coming out here? "Thanks, by the way. For, uh, the other day."

"No problem."

"I was so embarrassed," I add.

"Don't be. Hey, I've fallen in front of tens of thousands of people. Maybe hundreds of thousands. Millions."

Millions? What? Does this guy have an enormous ego, or is he delusional? I have no idea what he's talking about.

It must show on my face, because he says, "You know, on the ice."

"On the ice?"

He raises his eyebrows. "You *don't* know?"

"Hey, I just got here," I said. Could I have insulted him? For all I know, he's Japan's biggest pop star.

"When I'm skating," he clarifies. "I fall down a lot."

So that's it. The twirling. The spinning. He's a

figure skater. Does everyone know but me? Probably. I remember the way the girls at school were cooing over him, like he's some kind of celebrity. Maybe he *is* a celebrity.

"Do you skate competitively?"

He shrugs again. "I did before. But now it doesn't seem so important."

I get what he means. Watching TV, seeing all those people in shelters standing in line for water, makes me realize how selfish I am. I keep thinking about Yamada, that tomato farmer who lost his whole family. My problems and concerns seem so unimportant in the grand scheme of things. Who cares if I become Raoul's legal daughter or not? Who cares if everybody thinks I'm Junpei's cousin? At least I have people who care about me, who aren't floating around in the ocean somewhere.

I want to ask Taiga about the earthquake, about how it feels to move away from home, about what it's like to spin on ice, but I don't want to spoil the mood. Another time.

"So how do you like it here?" he asks.

"It's nice." I wish I could tell him how cold Obaachan has been, and how weird it was to learn that I had another sister. Somehow, it seems like he'd understand. But blurting out all of my secrets during our first private conversation might be a little too American. "It's confusing," I amend.

He gives me a crooked smile. "No doubt. People here are pretty conservative. I spent a lot of time in Canada with my skating coach. It always takes time to adjust to how different everything is here when I come back." He points to my sketchbook. "What's that?"

"I was going to draw something."

"Are you an artist?" There's a teasing note in his voice, but I want him to take me seriously.

"Yeah, something like that. I draw manga."

"Cool. Can you show me?"

I'm about to hand my notebook over when I remember the sketches that I did of him. What if he recognized himself? How embarrassing would that be? What if he thought I was some kind of stalker chick?

"These are rough." I hug my notebook to my chest. "But I could give you a copy of my manga story."

"Cool."

I could stand here and talk to him forever. Even after everything he must have been through, there's something strong and confident about him. He's calm. Solid. Not all unpredictable like my new family.

Then, almost as if I've conjured them up, Otosan and Mariko suddenly appear.

"There you are," my father says. "We looked everywhere for you."

I've been gone maybe ten minutes.

Taiga gives me a sympathetic smile.

"I woke up early," I say. "I just went for a little walk."

"We were so worried," Mariko adds.

About what? It's not like we're in a war zone or a crime-ridden city. There are no wild animals around or even any stray dogs, as far as I can tell. What could happen?

Mariko puts her arm around me and pulls me away from Taiga. They don't want me talking to the neighbors?

"See you later," I tell Taiga.

He gives me a little wave, turns, and jogs back down the road.

When he's gone, I follow Otosan and Mariko back to the house. "I promise I will never wander off without telling you again," I say. "Next time I will leave a note."

Frankly, I'm starting to feel a little claustrophobic. I realize that if I don't speak up for myself, I will start to feel like a prisoner. I want to have at least a little independence and make some plans of my own. After breakfast, while Otosan and I are still sitting at the table and Mariko is washing the dishes, I tell them about the manga club and the invitation to go to the anime studio on Saturday.

"Is it okay if I go?"

"Yes, of course," Otosan says. "Junpei can go with you."

"Oh, that's not necessary. He probably has plans of his own. I can figure out the bus."

"No, no. Junpei can take you. Or Mariko will drive you. Bus is all in Japanese. You might get off at the wrong stop or get lost."

"I have a phone with GPS. If I get lost, I'll call you. Or I'll call 119 if there's an emergency."

He frowns. Maybe he's thinking that he has to take care of me because of my disability, but he's too polite to bring it up. Little does he know that Mom lets me do stuff on my own all the time.

"Please, I really want to do this by myself. I'm starting to feel like a baby."

Finally, Mariko pipes up. "Oh, let her go."

Thank you, I mouth.

When Otosan at last gives his consent, she winks at me.

13

On Saturday morning, Mariko walks me to the bus stop and shows me how to read the timetable and tells me how much it'll cost. She waits until the bus looms into view. I hold up my arm, signaling it to stop. When it does, I climb aboard.

We've driven through the city on our sightseeing expeditions, so I have a basic idea of where everything is. Although at first I thought I'd take the bus all the way to the train station, where the manga club will gather to meet, I decide to get off a couple of stops early and explore a bit. If I'm on my own, no one will have to wait for me to catch up. I can limp along as slowly as I like. According to my phone, there's plenty of time.

When I step down to the sidewalk, I almost get mowed down by a girl in a navy skirt whizzing past on her bicycle. I wait at the curb for the signal to change. Different sounds chirp to indicate "Walk" or "Don't Walk." "Walk" is sort of like *pa po pa po*. I figure out that it's to help blind people know when to cross.

On the other side of the road is a veterinarian's office. A woman clutching a squirmy puppy gets out of her car. She's so busy with her ball of fur that she doesn't seem to notice me and my gimpy leg at all. I keep going until I reach a wooden bridge arching over a moat. A swan floats under the bridge, paddling in the murky water. Orange carp flash by. Willow trees line the sidewalk.

Over the bridge, I come to a park. According to a sign, there used to be a castle here—not the Disney kind with pointy towers and white turrets, but a Japanese castle, where the shogun lived. I try to imagine its curved roofs and white walls. I walk through the park till I get to a little mom-and-pop store advertising Pocari Sweat, which seems to be everywhere. Nearby, there's a set of steps going over the train tracks. I slowly climb up, hanging on to the railing to keep my balance. From above I can see the trains lined up in the train yard. One of them is painted with anime characters. I clatter down to the other side, pass a bank of bright red vending machines and a replica of Rodin's *The Thinker* sitting in front of a drugstore, and cross another street.

Some of the manga club members are waiting in

front of the train station. They're easy to find because they're wearing their school uniforms. Sora spots me and starts waving furiously.

I wave back. When the green man lights up, I cross the road and join them.

Yukiko takes a lace-trimmed handkerchief out of her purse and blots her forehead. "We walk," she says, pointing through the copse of skinny palm trees swaying in front of the station. Mt. Bizan hunches in the background. In between, there's a busy intersection flanked by lots of shops selling everything from shoes to flowers to pastries.

"Let's take a taxi," Sora says, with a glance at my leg.

The others murmur and nod. My face heats up, but I feel grateful. I don't want my gait to slow them down, after all. And it *is* hot.

I follow them to the head of the line of yellow cabs in front of the station. The back door of the first one opens automatically, as if by magic. Sora slides in the backseat first, then Reiko. I get in last. Yuma climbs into the front seat. The others set out on foot. Sora rattles off directions in Japanese, and the driver grunts in reply. I catch him checking me out in the rearview mirror.

"Later, let's go shopping," Sora says to me in English. "There's a manga store over there." She gestures to the left of the station.

I nod.

"*Amerika-jin, desu ka?*" the driver asks in a gruff voice.

"*Hai,*" Sora says, answering for me.

So much for blending in.

"No English," the driver says. "Only Japanese."

I guess he's saying that he doesn't speak English, which is fine. I don't get why everyone is so defensive about their language skills. After all, I'm here as a visitor to their country. I should be trying to speak their language. "*Daijobu,*" I say. It's okay.

We pull into traffic in the direction of the mountain. As it turns out, the anime studio isn't too far. It's just across a canal in which a few people are paddling around in kayaks. The driver lets us off at the entrance to a covered shopping arcade, next to a waterside Italian restaurant. Saho pays the fare. We wait on the corner for a few minutes until the others catch up.

"Have you ever heard of UFO Table?" Reiko asks me.

"No," I admit.

"Headquarters are in Tokyo," she says. "They set up office here for new ideas."

The three of them start talking in Japanese about some anime, which I figure out is produced by UFO Table. I don't understand everything, but the gist is that there's this town where everyone is born as a twin and something about girls with machine guns.

The others straggle toward us, their shirts blotched with sweat. Only Yukiko, who carries a ruffled parasol, looks remotely cool.

"Ready?" Emi leads the way down the boardwalk, past a sign that advises us to "Slip with Caution."

The UFO Table studio is just a few buildings down. There's a café on the first floor. We climb the stairs to a glass door where a young guy with a goatee and glasses is waiting for us. I check his hands and note that they are smudged with ink. He must be one of the creators.

Everyone bows—including me, albeit half a beat late—and says *"Yoroshiku onegai shimasu!"*

The guy introduces himself as Shun Tanaka and leads us on the grand tour, starting with the lobby with its posters advertising upcoming anime films. One appears to be about a group of young women on a pilgrimage. There's this circuit of eighty-eight temples, and at each temple people pray for something different, such as success on a school exam or fertility. Supposedly, lots of miracles have occurred along the way—people have been cured of various maladies— and there are stories about dragons and treasures. When Mom lived here she visited all eighty-eight temples, just for fun. She has a booklet with stamps from each temple.

Next, Shun takes us into the actual studio where several artists are busily sketching. They pause when we enter and bow their heads in greeting.

"Sometimes they make manga into movies," Sora says in a low voice. "You should show them *Gadget Girl*."

"You think?"

She nods. "You are very good at drawing."

I turn back to the room and try to figure out what Shun is saying. He gestures to one of the artists and points at a manga-style poster advertising Awa Odori, the summer dance festival in August when the spirits of the dead are supposed to return. The poster reminds me of all of the people who were swept away by the tsunami and the families and friends they left behind, still living in shelters, still grieving.

I watch the artist's pen fly over the paper and I get an idea. I may not be able to volunteer to rebuild or play soccer, but I can draw. I'm an awesome artist. I'm going to draw a picture and send it to Tohoku.

After the tour, we pose for a group photo. We bow in unison as we say good-bye to the artists and other staff of UFO Table. Shun shows us to the door.

"It would be so awesome to work there," I say as we clatter back down the stairs.

"Yes!" Sora agrees. "Or we could start our own manga studio. We could call it . . . Indigo Sky!"

"Not a bad idea."

We take a taxi back to the station and hit up the manga store before heading back home.

That evening, I check in with Whitney before calling Mom. I can't wait to tell her about my visit to a real live Japanese anime studio.

At first, her face fills the screen. "Hey, there. Can you guess where I am?" She pulls away so I can make out the edges of an indigo-dyed tapestry and a *Princess Mononoke* movie poster.

"Um, get out of my room!" I say with a laugh.

She flops on my bed, still holding her tablet. "I'm taking over your life. You might as well stay where you are."

I know she's kidding, but her words make me feel the tiniest bit uneasy. They have Whitney to babysit. They don't need me. "What's wrong with your life?"

"Well, for one thing, I don't have an awesome stepfather who's a culinary genius," she says. "Yesterday he sent me home with a pan of homemade lasagna, which I can assure you is way too labor intensive for my mother to bother with."

"Yes, he is a good cook," I concede. Before Raoul entered our lives, Mom and I subsisted mostly on frozen entrees and delivery pizza.

"I also don't have an adorable baby sister. And, *shhh*, don't tell your mom this, but I would totally babysit for free. Esme is that cute."

At the mention of my youngest sibling, I feel a pang of homesickness mixed with a dash of jealousy. Esme is probably starting to think that Whitney is her big sister, not me. Will she even remember me when I get back?

"How much are they paying you, anyway?"

"More than the movie theater." She has a part-time job selling tickets and popcorn at a Cineplex in Muskegon, but she considers it research for her future career as a Hollywood costume designer. "And how about you? Have you started a new manga story?"

"Uh, no. Not yet. I've been soaking up the culture, making some preliminary sketches."

She frowns.

To distract her, I start describing my field trip with the manga club to UFO Table, taking care to describe everyone's outfits in great detail.

"Sounds like you've made some new friends," Whitney says in a neutral voice.

Could she be jealous? I tamp down that thought. It occurs to me that even though I'm homesick and things have been a bit rocky, I want to spend more time here. I miss Whitney like crazy, but I don't want to leave my new family and my new friends. I want to hang out more with Sora. And Taiga. Also, I want to do something to help the people in Tohoku.

★ ★ ★

When Mom pops up on my screen for our scheduled chat, she looks a bit harried.

"I looked into flights. The soonest you can come back would be next Friday, and you'll have to change planes in Taipei and San Diego. It'll be a long flight but . . ."

"Hold on," I interrupt, suddenly overcome with guilt. Making phone calls and Internet searches has probably cost her studio time, not to mention the added stress of worrying about my unhappiness. "Things are better now. I want to stay."

"Oh." The crease between her eyebrows immediately disappears.

"Sorry for wasting your time," I mutter.

"No, no, that's okay."

At least I won't be wasting money. I know there would have been a hefty fee for changing my flight.

"So what changed your mind?"

"You did. You were right about everything. If I leave now, I may never get to know Otosan and Junpei. And Mariko."

"And your grandmother?"

"And my grandmonster. I mean, grandmother."

Plus, there's now the added attraction of Taiga. Not that he'd be interested in me. He probably has a celebrity skater girlfriend somewhere, but he's kind. Maybe we can be friends.

"Well, I'm glad. Grandma and Grandpa Cassidy

send their love, by the way. Grandma is mailing you some cookies."

"Give them my love back."

I start telling her about our sightseeing expedition. She nods enthusiastically every time I mention something that she visited herself back in the day. "And then did you drop by the Isamu Noguchi Museum?" Noguchi is one of her favorite sculptors. He was half Japanese like me—son of a famous Japanese poet and the American woman he hired as his secretary. He fell in love with the rocks in Shikoku and set up a studio here.

"Yeah, it was very peaceful," I say.

Just then there's a light knock on the door.

"Yes?"

The door slides open and Otosan peeks in. His eyes go to the screen, to Mom. They haven't seen each other, either in person or via computer, since Mom left Japan all those years ago. He freezes, as if in shock. A ripple of sadness and longing crosses his face. Is it possible that he never got over her? *Maybe he still loves her.*

I'm just about to invite him into the conversation when he mutters an "I'm sorry" and closes the door again.

Mom and I look at each other for a moment without speaking.

"Your dad," she says, finally.

"Yeah." I manage a chuckle. "That was pretty awkward, huh?"

"Tell him I said hello."

14

I spend the better part of the following afternoon drawing and shading with colored pencils. The final result is a serene-looking girl, who is actually me, with her eyes closed and hands together in prayer. All around her are images of happy, hopeful things such as a dove, a plant sprouting from the earth, a laughing baby. I use soothing colors, shades of blue and green, and soft lines. When I'm finished, I sign my name in the corner and show it to Mariko.

"How do you feel when you look at this picture?" I ask.

She studies it for a moment and decides upon "Peaceful."

Good. That's the effect I was going for. If someone up north looks at this and feels peaceful or calm even for a few seconds, then maybe I will have contributed to the relief effort somehow.

I put the picture in the futon closet where it will be flat and safe until I'm ready to mail it.

* * *

"Would you like to help us with the indigo tomorrow?" Otosan asks later that evening.

"Instead of going to school?"

I spent an entire year obsessing about indigo. I planted a seed in a little terra-cotta pot back in Michigan and treated it like a pet. I read books and scoured websites and asked questions at the local nursery, just so I could be a good plant parent. And I wrote reports on indigo for school assignments. I did all this because I wanted to impress my indigo farmer father whom I had yet to meet. Now, here I am, Indigo Girl herself, invited to step up and lay claim to my heritage and all I want to do is go to school.

"Yeah, sure," I say. "That would be great."

Otosan doesn't know me well enough to figure out that my enthusiasm is fake. I'm glad. I know he's making an effort, and I really do want to learn more about indigo farming and get to know my father and Mariko better. It's just that I think I've found my muse.

"Did you know that indigo production in America started in South Carolina?" I ask my father.

We're bumping down the road in his little white truck on our way to the field.

He glances over at me. "No, I didn't know."

"Africans who were brought over as slaves were growing indigo on this plantation that was managed by a seventeen-year-old girl named Eliza Pinckney," I continue, happy to share my wealth of indigo knowledge.

He looks at me again, his gaze resting a little longer this time. "Is that something you'd be interested in? Managing an indigo farm?"

I can't tell if he's serious or not. Obviously, I don't want to be a slave owner. Farming is too much for just one person so I'd have to hire people to help. I'm not sure that I would put myself in charge of some enterprise.

"Let me try it out first," I say, going for a jokey tone. "Let me see how I like it."

"Your mother didn't like it too much," he says, all serious, his eyes back on the road.

My ears perk up, and I wait for him to say more, but he falls into a brooding silence. All my life, I've been told that Mom left Japan to raise me by herself in the States because my father's parents rejected us. They wouldn't accept Mom because she was American and me because I was disabled. That's what she always said, anyway. But now I'm wondering if there was more to it than that. Maybe Mom left because she didn't want to live and work on my father's ancestral land. Maybe she rejected them.

Thinking about this makes me feel a mix of shame and guilt. I feel a flicker of sympathy for my father. Well, today I'll work hard. Maybe during this vacation I can start to make up for what my mother did to him.

We go past a cluster of little shops, a convenience store, and a yakitori stand. Then Otosan veers off the road onto a dirt two-track. He parks within sight of a patch of shin-high plants, green as grass. The indigo field. We climb out of the truck.

The harvest has already begun. About half of the plants have been cut down, the leaves spread over a couple of sheets of blue tarp.

"Can you use a sickle?" Otosan holds up a curved blade for my inspection. He gestures cutting a stalk with the tool. "If you work close to the plants, you won't cut yourself."

I nod thoughtfully. "I'll try."

I follow him to the field and watch as he cuts some leaves.

It's too hard for me to crouch, so I kneel at the edge of the field, grab a stalk with my good hand, anchor it with my knee, and saw gently with the sickle, leaving enough stem for more leaves to grow. I toss the leaves into a plastic yellow bin.

My shoulders tighten and tense while I'm working, so I stop every now and again to stretch.

Otosan does the same. We work silently, and at first I think it might be nice to have a radio out here blasting music, keeping us company, but then I start to enjoy the sound of the wind rustling the plants, the cicadas, the birds twittering in the trees. Every once in a while, Otosan looks over, probably checking to make sure I haven't cut myself. Then he smiles and goes back to work.

When I've filled up the bin, I call him over.

"Nice work," he says. "Want to help me carry it over?"

I grab onto one side of the bin, and he takes the other. We heave it to one of the blue sheets and dump the leaves out to crisp in the sun.

"The weather's supposed to stay good through the weekend," he says. "They'll be ready for stomping soon."

In South Carolina, slaves were forced to harvest and process the indigo. It's a lot of work, not something that one person can do easily alone. After the Civil War, people stopped growing indigo in the South.

"Do you always do this by yourself?" I ask him.

"No, we farmers help each other. If you want to, you can invite some of the kids you met at school," he says.

I imagine us all barefoot, tramping around in the

leaves, as if we were making wine or something. Or kicking through the maple and oak leaves that pile up on the sidewalk in Michigan in autumn. Anyway, it sounds like fun.

15

For the next few days, I help Otosan with the indigo. When we gather for dinner, my grandmother looks at me differently, as if she's changed her mind about me. For the first time ever, she refills my empty glass with cold barley tea and gestures to my rice bowl.

"No, thank you," I say, putting my hand over the top of it. "I've had enough." Still, I'm moved that she's thinking of me, trying to please me. She seems impressed by my hard work, which makes me wonder if Mom was a slacker when she was here in Japan. Maybe she avoided cutting indigo plants and washing dishes. For all I know, the animosity between my grandmother and Mom had nothing to do with race or nationality or my disability. I can imagine my mother excusing herself from chores to heed the higher calling of her art, and I'm pretty sure that wouldn't have gone over well with Obaasan.

Although I'm just getting the hang of farming, Otosan suggests that I go to school with Junpei for the last week of classes. It gives me a chance to see Sora and Taiga and invite them to the indigo stomping party that I've cooked up and my father has agreed to. On the last day of school, everyone gathers in the gymnasium again for the Closing Ceremony. Once again, I sit in a folding chair on the sidelines and Taiga is called upon to translate for me.

"The principal is telling everyone to be careful while riding their bicycles," he whispers.

His arm brushing against mine raises goose bumps.

"And now the principal is reminding everyone to keep up with their studies."

This time, I don't have to go onstage or even say good-bye. Most of the students keep their eyes trained forward. At the end of the ceremony I remind Taiga of the party, prepared to tamp down my disappointment if he's changed his mind.

"I'll be there," he says.

I feel a whoosh of joy.

The next time I call Mom, I ask to talk to Raoul.

"Sure, hold on," she says, and calls his name.

He comes sprinting into view. "What's up, buttercup?"

I roll my eyes.

"Okay, then. Aiko."

"I have a favor to ask."

"Another plant to water?" He claps a hand to his forehead in mock despair. Last year when we went to Paris, I'd left him in charge of the sprig of indigo that I was trying to grow. He did his best (he says), but it wilted in my absence.

"No. This is for something that you're actually good at."

"You want me to cook something?"

I note that he's wearing an apron. I must have interrupted breakfast-making. Suddenly, I have a huge craving for his huevos rancheros. There's nothing like tortillas and eggs with salsa in the morning.

"I need you to make me a playlist." I explain about the leaf-crunching party that I have in mind.

"So . . . songs that have something to do with indigo or the color blue?"

"Yeah, that would be perfect. And maybe add that grape-harvesting song you played on your radio show a while back."

He gives me two thumbs up. "You got it."

I feel a little bit bad about not spending more time with Junpei. What with the manga club and the indigo, I've been a little busy. I haven't been the big sister I'd promised myself I'd be. On the first day of summer vacation, I find him sprawled across the living room tatami watching high school baseball on TV.

"Hey," I call out by way of greeting.

"Hey." He perks up suddenly. "Do you want to see my new robot?"

"Sure." I follow him up the stairs to his room. A metal contraption sits in the center of the room surrounded by wads of paper.

"You can sit there," he says, gesturing to the chair in front of his desk. I step around clumps of paper and have a seat.

"What does it do?" I ask. The thing looks like it's made of an Erector Set.

"Wait. You'll see." He climbs onto his bed and grabs a remote control from deep within the covers. When he pushes a button, the robot begins to whir and move. At first, it slides back and forth, as if it's just warming up, but then it extends and bends. Pincers open and close upon a balled-up piece of paper. The robot scoots over to the wastebasket and drops the paper in.

"This is brilliant!" I slap my bare leg with my right hand to make a clapping sound. I have no idea how he created this thing, but I'm impressed.

Junpei beams. "This is for our school competition. If I win, I can go to the next level."

"Is this your first robot?"

He shakes his head, turns on the laptop that's on his desk, and brings up some YouTube videos. First, we watch scenes from last year's high school robotics competition where a somewhat shorter and skinnier Junpei tries to coax his robot upright after it falls over. Then we watch some winning high school robots stacking blocks and carrying eggs over hilly terrain.

"And check out these!" he says, bringing up images of a sophisticated robotic apparatus used to help elderly people pick fruit from high branches and one Transformers-type suit that enables people with paralyzed legs to walk upright.

"Maybe you can create a robot to help out with the indigo," I crack.

Junpei doesn't get that it's a joke. His face goes all serious. "That's my dream."

"Hmmm." Even though I'm not so sure that I would want to spend all of my time harvesting leaves and stirring dye, I like the idea that some people are still doing all that by hand. After all, if it's easy and mechanical that people want, they can use chemical dyes. Not that robots aren't useful. It would be great to have a robot like the one Junpei has made to clean my room, and I know that robots were sent into the nuclear power plant in Fukushima after the meltdown. And there's that robot rambling over Mars and sending back footage.

"You know, I think you should throw yourself into making robots," I say. "Forget about the indigo."

He shakes his head. "I'm the *chonan*." Eldest son. "And we're one of the last families to grow indigo here. My grandfather was a Living National Treasure because of his indigo dyeing. We have to carry on the tradition."

"Well, I admire your 'filial piety,'" I say, throwing in an expression I learned from a short story I read. "But it's your life."

He is quiet for a moment, putting words together in his head. I can almost see the thoughts roiling underneath, rippling his forehead. "Do you want to take over the farm?" Hope flashes across his features, lifting his shoulders.

I chuckle in spite of myself. "No, I don't think so."

"Then I have no choice. There's no one else."

"Oh, Junpei." I think of all of those people in shelters up in the northeast, people who've lost everything they ever had, like the guy who grew tomatoes. "We'll think of something."

I remember that I have yet to mail the picture that I drew. I'm still pretty much illiterate in Japanese, so I need help with the addresses.

"Could you do me a huge favor?" I ask my brother. "I want to snail mail something to one of the shelters up north. Could you help me find an address? And a postage stamp?"

It takes him about ten minutes to come up with the address of a group that is getting ready to go up to the disaster zone with supplies. I figure I'll take a chance and send it to the leader. Junpei writes down the kanji for the aid group and for this house. He even produces a large manila envelope and some stamps.

It's not much, just a piece of paper with some lines drawn on it, but maybe it'll do some good. I schlep down the street to the postbox and stick the envelope inside.

16

Although I check my e-mail compulsively over the next couple of days, there's nothing from Raoul. Oh, well. Maybe he forgot.

The evening before our indigo crushing party, just before dinner, I check again. Voila! I've received a file titled "Songs in the Key of Blue."

"Thank you, thank you!" I say out loud.

My laptop makes a sound that indicates there's an incoming video call. It's Raoul, still online. I glance at the time. It must be four a.m. over there.

I click to answer the call.

He shows up on my screen all bleary-eyed. His chin and cheeks are peppered with whiskers.

"What are you doing, getting up so early?" I ask him.

"I haven't gone to bed yet." He suppresses a yawn.

"Did Esme keep you up all night?"

"Au contraire. Last night was about the only night she slept through, which finally gave me a chance to put these tunes together for you. There's about an hour's worth of music there. Is that enough? Should I come up with more?"

I can't believe he stayed up all night just to make a mix for the indigo stomping party. Wow! My throat knots up for a second because I'm so moved by his kindness, and then I'm overcome with guilt for keeping him awake all night. And for not being a better, more devoted stepdaughter.

"You didn't have to stay up all night," I say. "But thanks. You're the best."

"Hey, I wanted to." He shrugs as if it's no big deal, but I know that it is.

"I owe you. Big time."

"Just give me a hug when you get back, and we'll call it even."

"Okay. I can do that."

"And a fist bump."

I laugh. "I can do that, too."

I wait till after dinner and a bath to download the songs. I listen to them on my iPod, in the dark, on my futon. I don't look at the titles at first, just let the music wash over me. The first song has a nice beat and makes me bob my head. It segues into a tune by a woman folksinger, followed by a guy singing about "no blue skies." Some of the selections are instrumental.

The very last song, however, doesn't seem to be

about the color blue at all. I recognize the voice as that of Paul Simon. It has a South African vibe. He's singing about a girl having a bad dream, and a golden retriever standing guard. I give in and peek at the title: "Father and Daughter." Ah. A bonus track. A secret message. I blink away tears. I owe him another hug and another fist bump.

The next morning, Junpei and I help to unload the bins of dried leaves onto a blue plastic tarp spread out in the barn. We've just unloaded the last bin when the guests begin to arrive. First, Sora shows up wearing a homemade skirt modeled after a manga character's costume. Then comes Taiga looking gorgeous in jeans and a T-shirt. Lastly, Good appears from next door with Chika on her hip.

Good plops the baby down on a blanket and hands her a toy. It's one of those shape sorters, where you have to fit blocks into holes. She becomes engrossed, barely noticing when her mom steps away and onto the blue tarp scattered with dried indigo leaves.

I crank up the music—"Blue Monday" by New Order—and slip out of my shoes. The leaves crunch under my feet. Our job is to break the leaves off of the stems.

"Great song," Taiga says.

"I got my stepfather, Raoul, to make a playlist," I tell him. "He's a DJ in America."

"Kakkoi!" Good's eyes widen.

Okay, it sounds cooler than it is. He doesn't spin discs in a club. He actually hosts a world music show on public radio, but I don't say this. I want everyone to be impressed with my stepfather, the guy who is happy to claim me as his daughter.

"Blue Monday" is dance music. Good starts moving her hips and waving her arms. What the heck. I throw in some moves of my own. Junpei continues stomping as before, pretending to ignore us, the crazy foreigners. But my father smiles slightly, and Mariko nods her head in time to the music.

By the time the song segues into "Mo' Better Blues," Taiga has joined in.

Chika has finished her puzzle. Now she's watching us, clapping her hands together, enjoying the show.

"Let's make a conga line," I say. The music is making me feel bold. I want to get everyone involved. We can pulverize these leaves and have fun at the same time.

"What's a conga line?" Sora asks.

I look over at Taiga. He nods and comes closer, then turns his back to me. I put my right hand on his shoulder. I can't quite manage to get my left hand up there. "Do like this," I say.

I feel Mariko's fingers flutter and settle onto my shoulders. Good is next, and then my father. Sora joins as well.

"Come on, Junpei," Taiga says in English.

At first, I think my brother is going to bolt out the door, but he finally shuffles over and takes his place at the end of the line, his hands on Sora's shoulders.

"Ready?" Taiga calls out.

"Yes!"

We start snaking slowly around the tarp. I'm concentrating on the movement of my feet, but I'm aware of my hand on Taiga's shoulders, the muscles rippling beneath my fingers, the heat of his body. I'm close enough to catch the clean-laundry scent of his T-shirt and the faint aroma of sweat and skin.

Left foot forward, right foot forward.

I can feel Mariko's breath on my neck as she laughs softly.

Suddenly, Good's voice rings out. "Stop! Someone take a video!"

There is such urgency in her voice that we all turn toward her. Good is looking at Chika, who has managed to get up onto her feet.

She gurgles and claps, seeming to be delighted to be the focus of our attention.

Junpei and Taiga both whip out their cell phones and aim them at Chika.

"Da! Da!" she says. And then, as if she's been waiting for the filming to start, she takes a step toward Good. Left foot, then right foot, then left foot again.

She keeps stumbling onward until she collapses into her mother's outstretched arms.

"Got it!" Junpei says and promises to send the footage to Good later.

We all start to clap.

My throat knots and tears cloud my vision. I have just witnessed Chika's first steps.

A long time ago, Mom recorded my own first steps. She used to take a video camera along to my physical therapy sessions so that she could record my progress. At first, like most babies, I could only walk while seated in a walker with wheels. When I was about three, I graduated to one without a seat, and then that same year to one of those tubular frames that elderly people use, and then to crutches. At four, I managed to take a few steps while holding my physical therapist's hands. And then she let go. I moved my left foot forward, my right foot forward, and . . . fell. I still fall sometimes.

Good is trying to get Chika to walk again, but she burrows against her mother, suddenly shy.

Obaasan shows up just then with a tray laden with glasses of barley tea and sliced pears on a plate. For once, her face is creased into a smile, her eyes lost in crinkles. It must make her happy to see the indigo being processed, the continuation of her family's history.

"Let's take a break," my father says.

We brush off our feet and move away from the tarp.

Obaasan holds the tray out in my direction. *"Dozo."*

I hunch my head and shoulders forward in a sort of a bow and take a glass. *"Arigato gozaimasu,"* I say, thanking her politely.

My father hangs back, taking a look at what we've done so far and nods. Obaasan says something to him. He picks up a glass, downs the tea in a few gulps, and grabs a rake. While the rest of us sit on the sidelines munching pears, he begins to separate the stems from the leaves, first with the tines of the rake, and then by squatting and using his hands.

I feel guilty just watching him, so I quickly finish my drink and join in.

"Where's Junpei?" Sora asks, crouching down next to me.

Junpei, I notice, has left the barn. I shrug apologetically. "He's not all that crazy about this indigo business," I tell her. Maybe this year I can give him a break. Instead of tending the leaves and the dye, he'll have more time to dream about robots and play baseball with his friends.

"What do we do next?" I ask.

"So, desu ne." My father slowly draws out his words, but his fingers are quick and deft. "Next, we

will compost these leaves. We will spray them with water and turn over the leaves. Do you think you can do that?"

Sounds easy enough. "Sure."

The dried leaves are black, dead, but they will change cloth to the color of the sky. Already I am thinking about what I will dye in the vat: a scarf for Whitney, a baseball cap for Raoul, a shawl for my mother. But it'll be another month or so.

I hear a rustle of leaves and then Taiga is beside me. He plucks a few stems from the pile and tosses them off to the side. Then the music segues from Joni Mitchell to an instrumental piece. Taiga becomes still, listening. "What is this song?" he asks me.

I cock my head and tune in for a moment. Horns blare and violins swell. This melody always makes me think of cars driving around Broadway in New York City. "'Rhapsody in Blue,'" I tell him. "It's by George Gershwin."

"Hmmm." He nods thoughtfully and resumes sorting, but more slowly this time, as if he is concentrating on the music.

When the song is over, he turns to me and says, "Hey, do you want to meet up tomorrow and chase down the bakery truck?"

My heart does a flip. Is he asking me on a date? "Yeah, sure." I resist grabbing handfuls of leaves and throwing them into the air like confetti.

17

The next morning, after flagging down the Donkey Bakery Truck, Taiga and I are sitting on the riverbank eating melon-flavored buns, talking about ice.

Ice is not my favorite thing. In fact, it's high on the list of things I hate, somewhere between earthquakes and middle school bullies. A lot of Michigan natives dislike ice. It's dangerous even for people who don't tend to fall down. Back in fifth grade, my teacher hit a patch of black ice and skidded across the median into the path of a semi. My first funeral.

Icicles glinting in the sunlight can be pretty, but ice isn't something I want to put my feet on. When I tell Taiga that I've never been ice skating before, he doesn't believe me.

"And don't tell me it's because of your disability," he says. "I've seen the Paralympics."

Yeah, me too. And people are always sending me inspirational videos of athletes with special needs—one-legged alpine skiers and blind marathon runners.

"Michigan is right up there next to Canada," he says, drawing a map in the air with his finger. "Doesn't everybody play hockey and go sledding and have snowball fights?"

I shake my head. "Not me. My mother isn't very athletic. She only wanted us to paint or listen to music." We go to plays and movies sometimes, but never to sports events. In winter, she makes cocoa and we huddle under a quilt together, reading books. When I was very small, we did go down a snow-covered sand dune on a plastic saucer, but I could tell that she was doing it just for me so I'd have that essential childhood experience, not because she thought it was a good time herself.

"That's it, then," he says.

"What?" The end of the conversation? The end of our friendship?

"I'm taking you ice skating."

"Here?" I make a show of checking out our surroundings. The cicadas are screeching. The sun is beating down on us. His face is shiny with sweat. There's no ice in sight.

"No." He reaches over and pinches my nose once, quickly, as if I'm a little kid. "There's a rink in Takamatsu. It's about an hour from here by train."

Well, it would be nice to get away from this heat. And to watch him skate. I think back to that morning when I first saw him spinning and twirling in the yard. A dervish. A ninja boy.

"Okay, I'll go. Just to watch."

He shakes his head. "You're going to skate. And we're leaving Saturday morning."

On Friday morning, Mariko is out when the doorbell rings. Obaasan is sitting before the family altar as usual at this time of day. She and Kana are no doubt in the midst of some deep supernatural conversation. She'd probably appreciate it if I got the door.

I schlep myself to the entrance. *"Hai?"*

The door slides open. It's the mail carrier. He holds out an envelope that was too big to fit into the mailbox and a few smaller letters. I accept them with my good hand.

After he's closed the door and taken off on his mail scooter, I drop the letters on the table. I notice that the big envelope is addressed to me. I press it against the table with my left arm, tear the edge off with my right hand, and shake out the contents. A sheet of white paper floats to the table. It's a one-page manga story. The first panel depicts a young man looking out at the sea. He's alone, standing at the edge of a cliff. Is he about to jump? Is he thinking about it? In the next panel, he's standing in line with a jerry can, waiting to fill it with water. Off to the side, there's a bulletin board with photos of the missing, messages, and phone numbers. Close up of an image of a girl praying. Around her head there are flowers, hearts, and doves. The young man's expression softens. He looks up toward the sun.

My heart starts beating faster as I realize that this is a reply to my drawing. Someone was actually moved by my work. If his illustrations are saying what I think they are, I may have even saved him from doing something drastic. I quickly turn over the envelope. Yes, there's a return address. And a name.

I immediately get to work on my reply. This time I make it more personal. I draw myself split in half, one family on each side. On the left, there is a map of America. On the right, a map of Japan. I draw the things that I love—manga, an indigo plant, a cup of hot chocolate. This time I don't show my drawing to Mariko. I don't even tell her about it. This is just between a lonely boy in Tohoku and me.

That night my father says, "The *sukumo* is ready. Tomorrow we are mixing the dye. Do you want to help?"

I notice that Obaasan has perked up at the mention of an indigo-related Japanese word. She looks straight at me, daring me with her eyes.

I know that this is one of the major steps in the

production of indigo. The leaves have been fermented, and now they're ready to be mixed with lye, wood ash, sake, and lime. Everything has to be just right, or the color won't turn out. This would be a good opportunity for a future master dyer to learn about the process.

"Um, actually I have plans to go ice skating with Taiga tomorrow."

Obaasan asks him what I said, and he translates my words into Japanese. My response was obviously the wrong one, because her face crumples into a scowl. She mutters something under her breath. I catch the words "mother" and "identical." *Just like her mother.*

Okay, I get it. She thinks I'm blowing off the all-important family business for my selfish pursuit of fun. Don't I get a break once in a while? This is my summer vacation, and Otosan and Mariko don't seem to mind.

"That sounds wonderful," Mariko pipes up from behind the counter.

My father nods. "Yes, you will have a good time."

Only Junpei is silent. I guess there's no way he can get out of it, being the eldest son and heir to the farm. I try to catch his eye, to give him a sympathetic look, but he excuses himself from the table and skulks to his room.

After dinner, I help clear the table, and then settle in with Otosan to watch the evening news.

This evening there is a story on the news about a nineteen-year-old man who worked in a nursing home. He was looking after patients when the tsunami warning went out. He took charge of a ninety-year-old woman, pushing her wheelchair up the hill as the wave approached.

In Hollywood movies, the weak often encourage the young and strong to go on ahead because they have the best chances for survival. In a movie, the ninety-year-old woman would have said, "Leave me. I've lived a long life. You are young! Save yourself!" But the young man said that he never thought of leaving the old woman.

"If Kayoko was going to die, I was going to go down with her," he said.

Obviously, they made it. Now they are both onscreen, Kayoko in her wheelchair, the young man beside her, patting her liver-spotted hand.

The reporter leans toward the woman. "Do you remember what happened?" he asks her.

She waves the microphone aside and shakes her head.

"Most of the time she doesn't even remember my name," the young man says with a laugh.

I can't help wondering if the boy who drew the

pictures knows these people, if he is hovering some-where in the background.

The next morning, Obaasan ignores me. She seems testier with Mariko than usual, which makes me feel a little guilty. I get the feeling that she's taking her irritation with me out on her daughter-in-law.

After she's settled in front of the altar, Mariko gives me a lift to the train station. When I get out of the truck, I see Taiga standing next to the vending machine out front, a carrying case in his hand. He waves with his other and bounds down to meet me.

"Have a good time," Mariko says with a knowing smile.

"Thanks. See you tonight at dinner." She lingers for a moment, but I wave her off. We watch her disap-pear in a cloud of dust.

Since this isn't the main station, just a stop along the way, there are few passengers on the platform. In fact, there's just an elderly guy, flapping a paper fan at his face, and a mother and child, holding hands.

"I got your ticket already," Taiga says. He reaches into his jeans pocket and produces a small piece of paper.

"Thanks." I nod toward the bag. "What's in there?"

"My skates."

"Oh. Of course."

A clanging starts up, and the gates come down. We can't see the train yet, but it's clearly on its way, so we line up on the platform. The little boy presses himself against his mother's front and peers around to spy on me.

"Hi there." I smile, but he frowns and pulls away. A few seconds later, I catch him looking again.

What does he see that's so different? Is it my chestnut-streaked hair? My eyes the color of pale tea? My stiff, twisted arm? I try to come up with a phrase, something to prove that I'm harmless and human, but his mother catches him staring and yanks him out of view. She gives him a sharp reprimand then looks over her shoulder at me and says, "I'm sorry my boy."

"It's okay," I tell her. "Really."

The train—all two cars of it—pulls up just then. When it comes squeaking to a stop, the elderly man gets on first, followed by the mother and child. Taiga and I board last and flop down in a booth facing each other. Happily, the interior is air-conditioned.

"When's the last time you went skating?" I ask Taiga. I imagine him taking this train every afternoon with that bag in his hand.

He looks out the window. "That day," he says.

Suddenly, he seems far, far away from me, sucked into the black hole of memory, and I could kick myself for wrecking the mood. I try to think of a joke, an anecdote, anything at all to get us out of this moment and back into the carefree happiness of five minutes ago.

"I was in the rink as usual, warming up to K-pop. My coach was leaning over the wall, yelling out advice. I was feeling really loose and happy, like I was invincible. I was totally in the zone." His face softens, lights up. "Without even really thinking about it, I threw my body into a spin. I was whirling like a top—once, twice, three times, and then four! I'd never managed four rotations before without falling, but this time I nailed it!"

I listen breathlessly. The scene is so vivid.

"My coach started jumping up and down and punching the air. At first, I thought that his jumping was making the building move, as totally irrational as that would have been. Then I heard the rafters creaking and I realized that we were having an earthquake."

A gasp escapes me. I grip the handrest and wait for him to go on.

"The ice shattered beneath my feet. I didn't know what to do. There was nothing to hide under. I tried to skate toward the exit, but chunks of the ceiling started raining down. I made myself into a ball and covered my head with my arms until the earth stopped moving. I thought I was going to die."

"But you got out!" I said, eager to hear the happy ending.

"Yes. I crawled on my hands and knees through the debris and I found an opening." He looks at me. "There was a little boy buried under plaster. When I dug him out, he was unconscious. I dragged him across the ice and out of the building. He woke up a little while later and he didn't remember anything about the earthquake at all."

"Was there . . . anyone else trapped inside?"

"No," he says. "The ones who were able helped the little kids get out. Everyone was fine."

He shrugs and smiles. Even though he's too modest to say so, I know that he was a hero on that day.

18

When we get to the rink, Taiga shoulders the door open. Cool air seeps out of the building. I hurry inside, away from the heat.

In Michigan, no one ice skates in summer. At least not where I'm from. Hockey sticks go into the back of closets or sheds. People switch to roller blades, tennis rackets, or surfboards. But why? I'm so relieved by the chill that suddenly nothing else makes sense. Summer is the perfect time to visit ice.

The rink is busier than I expected. Lots of little kids are stumbling around in circles. Some are hanging on to mothers' hands. A few glide in figure eights.

I follow Taiga to the counter where a girl drums her fingers impatiently.

"What size do you wear?" Taiga asks over his shoulder.

"Seven."

He frowns. "What's that in centimeters?"

"I don't know." I sit down on one of the benches in the lobby and take off one shoe, hoping it doesn't smell too bad. "Maybe you could hold it up to the other skates and compare."

He takes the shoe, holds it like a gift, and presents it to the girl at the counter with both hands. He explains something in Japanese, and they both look over at me.

I don't really want to skate. It's enough to sit here in the cool, not falling. But when Taiga comes back to me with a pair of white leather skates and kneels to work one of them onto my foot, I feel like Cinderella.

"I can do that," I say, embarrassed. His hands on my ankle send sparks all the way to my hairline.

"You have to tie them tightly," he says.

I'm not going to be attempting anything fancy. No triple toe loops or double salchows, whatever those are. I'll consider simply getting into the rink an accomplishment.

I take over the putting on of my own skates.

Taiga sits down beside me and takes a pair of black skates out of his bag. The blades are clean and shiny, but the leather looks worn.

"How many pairs do you have?"

"Just two. But they're custom-made, and I need a new pair every couple of months."

Wow. That must be expensive.

He laces them slowly and carefully, like a ritual.

When we're both in skates, he stands up and holds out his hand. "Are you ready?"

I grab on and let him pull me up. "Yeah, okay. Let's do this thing."

Taiga steps onto the ice first. I steady myself with knuckles against the wall. He holds out both hands. I take one, then the other, trying not to think too much about his skin touching mine. Instead, I focus on my feet. I plant my right foot, which is more stable than my left, onto the ice. Then I shift my weight a little, bring my left foot around, and . . . bam! We're both down.

"Sorry!" I knew this would happen, but tears fill my eyes.

"It's okay." Taiga gets up first, brushes a few crystals from his hip, braces himself, and yanks me into a standing position. He's steadier now, feet apart, prepared. He skates backwards, slowly, and I slide forward.

At first, he's just pulling me while I try to stay steady. I do my best to ignore the little girl spinning to our left as if there's nothing to it and the young mothers in short flippy skirts who fly past.

"Good, good," Taiga says, just before letting go.

I keep moving forward. I'm skating! I'm Mao Asada! I'm Gracie Gold! And then, of course, I fall again.

After half an hour of this, I know that my hips will

be mapped with bruises. My elbow will probably ache for days. But I manage to stay upright a little longer each time.

"Cocoa break?" Taiga suggests after my tenth or fifteenth sprawl.

"Okay, but then I want to see you skate."

We haul ourselves off the ice and to one of the little tables situated around the rink. I sit while Taiga goes to the vending machine. He returns with steaming paper cups. We sip, listening to the music mixed with children's laughter.

"So how old were you when you first started? Like this?" I gesture to a girl who looks around five.

"I was three."

"Wow." At three, I was going to physical therapy. "Did you ever want to try other sports?"

He shrugs. "Not really. But I played baseball for a little while, just to make my dad happy."

"There's another sport that I suck at," I joke.

"I wasn't very good at it, either," he says. "I spent a lot of time on the bench."

I look back at the rink and see that the girl who was spinning earlier is now soaring on one foot, the other extended behind her. She looks like a bird. She looks serious.

"Not bad," Taiga says, following my gaze. "But I bet she can't draw as well as you can."

"Thanks." I'd still trade drawing for skating. I'd

rather be able to run, leap, walk, without thinking too much about it, without ever falling down, than to "have a flair for discovering discerning details," as my art teacher once said.

Taiga drains his cup, leaving a sugary silt. He looks at me, eyebrows raised.

"Go." My cup is still half full. My bottom is sore. And I want to see what he can do. He deserves to have a little fun this afternoon.

"Okay. I'll be back."

I watch him take to the ice. Unencumbered, he is transformed. He glides like a swan on a lake, all grace and beauty. His legs move swiftly, confidently, and although he's just skating straight ahead, not doing any tricks, the twirling girl stops to watch. She grabs onto the wall and stands there, mesmerized.

The other skaters pause, too. The moms and the kids move aside like cars making way for an ambulance. A buzz starts up, and then a hush falls as Taiga gathers speed and jumps on the cleared ice. His skates grind up sparkles. It looks as if he's leaving a trail of fairy dust in his wake.

J-pop blares out of the speakers, some girl group singing about love. I'm sure it's not his usual music, but he makes do. He spins, twirls, leaps, muscle memory taking over. His skating is so smooth, so seamless. He skates figure eights and then gyres to the center and begins to spin, arms crossed over his chest, until he slows and comes to a complete stop. He reaches up one hand as if he's grabbing a star out of the sky, yanks it down, and finishes on one knee.

I start to clap. Pretty soon, the sound of applause and high-pitched squeals has drowned out the music. A couple of girls about my age skate up to him with notebooks and pens. If they'd had bouquets of flowers, they would have tossed them at his feet. After a few words, he scribbles in their notebooks. They're asking for his autograph because he's famous.

He spends several minutes greeting the skaters bold enough to approach him, bobbing his head as he absorbs their words of praise, when I'm sure all he wants to do is get back out there and skate some more. After he leaves the ice, the others finally resume skating and this time they are faster, more energetic, better.

As he comes closer, I see that his face is shiny with sweat. His chest is still heaving slightly, and there are dark patches under his arms.

"You made it look so easy," I say, watching a girl who'd been clinging to the wall before. Now, she is pushing toward the center, unafraid of the ice. "You're a magician. And you're famous."

He shakes his head vigorously, spraying me with sweat.

"Ew."

"The world of Japanese skating is very small,"

he says, dropping into the seat across from me. "Everyone knows each other."

"No, it's more than that. You totally inspired them." I wave toward the rink. One thing is absolutely clear: he can't give up skating. He doesn't need to shovel dead fish and build new houses. These people need him to spin and leap and nail those double salchows. "You have to go back to skating," I say. "Do it for Tohoku." Japan needs him. Maybe the whole world.

That evening, I give in to my curiosity and look him up on YouTube. I'm amazed by the number of hits that come up. Some of them are from years ago, when he was a little kid. There's one of him skating in a Santa costume with a fake white beard that floats like a cloud when he spins. I click on a more recent still of Taiga with a bandage wrapped around his head, wondering if it's another costume, some war drama on ice, maybe.

The video starts playing. Several male skaters in spangles and sparkles glide around a rink. None of them seem to be injured, even for pretend. In the background banners advertising multinational companies are plastered to the walls. The skaters are obviously warming up for a major competition.

Taiga comes into view, his arms outstretched as

if he is flying. He jumps and spins, and then changes course so that he's skating backwards. I can tell that he's in the zone, totally focused on his next move, almost as if he's forgotten that he's not the only one out there. He is clearly unaware of the skater in the faux tuxedo leotard coming toward him. I want to cry out "Be careful!" or "Fore!" I gasp as Taiga crashes into him backwards, at full speed. Both skaters go down, slamming their heads against the ice.

For a second, Taiga doesn't move, and even though I saw him today and he was fine, my stomach drops. He and the other guy are a pile of sprawled limbs, the blades of their skates glinting like knives. Soon, medics and coaches crowd around. I resist the urge to fast forward, past the fence of legs blocking my view. After a few moments, I catch a glimpse of his hand gesturing. A burly guy—his coach?—helps him onto his feet and supports him as he makes his way to the sidelines. Phew!

The video continues. The show must go on. All of the skaters, but one, clear the ice and the competition begins. First up is a skinny Italian with a ponytail, skating to a Beatles medley. He's good, but he doesn't have Taiga's spark.

Two more skaters follow, and then, to my amazement, the screen fills with Taiga's face. He now has a strip of white gauze pasted over his chin, and another wrapped around his head. I expect him to wave to his fans and make his exit, but unbelievably, he goes back out into the rink.

Once he's in his starting position, I hear the initial strains of Barber's "Adagio for Strings," which Raoul always says, half-jokingly, is the saddest music in the world. According to my stepfather, this music is the go-to composition for filmmakers who want to cue heartbreak. In this case, however, it becomes a song of triumph as Taiga skates through his program with a banged-up head. He lands badly on three of the jumps, falling again, as I did all afternoon, but he gets back up every time. He even manages one perfect triple-revolution spin.

After he's finished his program, he is showered with bouquets and stuffed animals. A roar fills the arena. The camera zooms in on spectators dabbing away tears. At the center of it all, Taiga scoops up a Hello Kitty doll, waves, and half-stumbles, half-skates to the wall, where he falls into his coach's arms. He can barely make it to the bench on the sidelines. As soon as he's heard his score, putting him at least temporarily in first place, he begins sobbing. A medic shows up with a gurney, and he manages a wavery smile for the camera before he is carried off and disappears from view. The picture goes blurry, but it's not because of the camera work. My eyes have filled with tears.

I do an Internet search to find out more. As it turns out, he needed stitches and weeks of rest. He had to withdraw from competition for a couple of months. It was probably not a good idea for him to skate after his collision, but his coach had reported that he didn't seem to have a concussion. He had wanted to skate no matter what, and so he did.

19

A couple of days later, I meet up with Sora at Starbucks. I want to tell her about buying bread and going skating with Taiga and maybe try to figure out why he hasn't made a move, but I can't seem to find the words. I'm not sure how girl talk works in Japan.

"Tell me," I nudge Sora with my shoulder. "Do you like my brother?"

She looks confused. "Your brother?"

Surely she knows that word. "Junpei!"

"Junpei is your . . . cousin, isn't he?"

Oh, right. "Yeah, my cousin. It's a figure of speech." I could clue her in, I guess, but the truth would be too confusing at this point. I lean over my drink and suck up iced matcha latte through the straw.

Sora accepts my explanation without comment. She looks down as she smooths her miniskirt across her lap and a blush rises to her cheeks. "Yes," she whispers.

"Does he know?"

She shakes her head quickly and waves her hands as if she's clearing the air of smoke.

"Well, I think you might have a chance," I persist. "I saw the way he was looking at you during the indigo stomping party. But as you told me, he's very shy. He won't make a move unless you do."

It takes a moment for her to sort out the meaning of my words. When she does, she peers into my eyes and asks, "So you think I should confess?"

"Confess? Did you do something bad?"

"No, no. Confess means confess to love."

This is the first time I've heard the *l* word since coming to Japan. I was starting to think that no one believed in it. Even so, I'm the last person to be giving advice to the lovelorn, but while I'm here I have to do what I can to help my brother.

"Well, I don't know if telling him directly that you love him is such a good idea. He might get scared. But you could invite him to go to karaoke or a festival with you. Maybe in a group?"

"Thank you, thank you." In her excitement, she grabs both of my hands, claw and all, and squeezes tightly. "That's a good idea!"

Mission accomplished. "Good luck!"

Now if only someone could give me a hint as to what I should do with my feelings for Taiga.

Back at the house, mindlessly doodling in my

sketchbook, I realize that the cousin thing is still bothering me. But who can I talk to about it? I've already mentioned it to Mom, and she wasn't much help. Whitney wouldn't understand. She's so proactive she'd probably push me to stage an intervention or something. And Sora? If I tell her that Junpei is actually my brother, the whole school will know and things might get really awkward for him. He can't up and leave at the end of summer like I can. I suppose I could talk to Good. As a foreigner, she'd probably be able to relate, but she's part of this neighborhood. I might be compromising her loyalty or something. The only person that I really want to discuss this with is Taiga. He's an outsider like me. He's been abroad, so he has a wider perspective. And something tells me that he's good at keeping secrets.

"I'll take the clipboard to the neighbor's house," I tell Mariko. "You know, with the memo about the neighborhood gateball tournament." I've noticed that it's still sitting on the shoebox in the entryway.

"Oh! Thank you." Mariko rustles in the refrigerator for a moment and comes up with a bag of eggplants. "Here, take these along with you. We've got more than we need."

So now I've got an excuse to drop in. I grab the bag and the clipboard, slide my feet into my shoes, and head for Taiga's uncle's house.

His aunt answers the door. When she sees my

face, she gets all flustered. "No English," she says. "Just a moment."

A few seconds later, Taiga is there in her place. He's wearing shin-length shorts with a green Hawaiian print and a white T-shirt that looks especially bright against his sun-bronzed skin. His hair is slightly damp, as if he's just gotten out of the shower. I smell soap.

"Hi!"

"I brought this." I hoist the bag of eggplants and jerk my chin at the clipboard tucked under my arm.

He relieves me of my burden and hands the stuff to his aunt, who hovers anxiously behind him.

I stand there for a moment, wondering what to do. Obviously he's not going to invite me inside. "So . . . do you want to go for a walk?"

"Yeah, sure. Hold on. Let me get my shoes."

We wander over to the riverside park and sit on the grassy embankment in view of Mt. Bizan. An archipelago of clouds wafts by overhead. Taiga leans back on his elbows, sitting with his legs extended. I sit cross-legged, even though I know that in Japan it's considered "man-style." We survey our surroundings in silence. A little kid in a floppy blue hat is running through the labyrinth below while his mom watches. Off to the left, small groups of senior citizens are making the rounds of the putting course.

Finally, I break the quiet. "Can I tell you a secret?"

He pulls in his knees. "Do I have to tell you one, too?" He forces a smile, but I can tell he's a little nervous.

"No. I just want you to listen. And not tell anyone what I'm about to tell you. Okay?"

"Okay." One leg stretches out in front of him.

"Do you remember how at the assembly the principal said that I was Junpei's cousin?"

He nods.

"Well, I'm not. I'm his sister—his half sister. Junpei's dad is my father."

For a second, Taiga is still, as if he's waiting for me to say more. Or maybe he's so shocked that he can't think of a reply.

"Is that it?" he asks softly. "Is that your secret?"

"Yes."

"Well, I hate to tell you this, but I think everyone already knows."

"But how?" Sora, for one, didn't know. And I'm sure that Junpei hasn't said anything. It's not as if we look so much alike, and that information isn't all over the Internet.

"Maybe the kids at school don't know, but my aunt and uncle remember your mother. They know that she got pregnant, and that she had a baby girl with special needs, and that she suddenly left. Apparently, it was quite the scandal."

"She was driven away," I say feebly. "We both

were." My instinct is to defend Mom, the one who brought me up on her own and taught me to be proud of myself, but now I'm wondering about the mess she left behind. Did she turn my father into a pariah? Did she shame my grandmother? Could that be the reason she hates Mom—and me—so much?

Taiga touches my shoulder. "Hey, it's not such a big deal anymore. We have a saying in Japan—after seventy days, everyone forgets. Anyway, on the outside, everyone pretends that they don't know. But as soon as you showed up, my aunt knew that you were the long-lost daughter, Aiko."

Inexplicable tears fill my eyes. I drag the back of my hand across my nose.

"A lot has happened since you and your mother were here," Taiga continues. "For a while, everyone was talking about how the Yamadas' eldest son had dropped out of Tokyo University and wouldn't leave his bedroom for a year. And then the Takahashis' son-in-law was arrested for embezzling to support his gambling addiction. You and your mother are pretty much old news."

When he turns to look at me, his eyes are full of warmth and tenderness. This is where we kiss, I think. This is where I close my eyes and he moves forward and our lips meet and the world falls away.

But no. He bumps his shoulder playfully against mine. "C'mon," he says, springing to his feet. "I hear the bakery truck making the rounds. Let's go get some melon bread."

He reaches down, grabs my hand, and pulls me up. Sadly, as soon as I'm on my feet, he lets go. I follow him over the hill.

20

It's already mid-August, time for Obon, one of the biggest Japanese holidays of the year. All over town I've seen the manga-style posters advertising Awa Odori, the summer dance festival in Tokushima.

"It's the biggest festival in all Japan," Sora tells me as we sit with our iced matcha lattes in a coffee shop at the mall. We've met up so that she can lend me a cotton *yukata* to wear to the festivities. "It's the Japanese Mardi Gras! People come from all over the country to dance in the streets. I'm going to dance with my *ren*. We've been practicing for the past six months." She twists her arms in the air, demonstrating.

I pull my cup closer to the edge of the table so that she doesn't accidentally knock it over. "Sounds like fun," I lie.

Dancing is not one of my talents. Especially not dancing while wearing wooden *geta* sandals, which are part of the Awa Odori costume, along with a cotton kimono and a hat made of straw. But Mariko tells me later that I won't have to.

"We have tickets for tomorrow night," she says during dinner. "We can sit in the bleachers and watch the dance troupes parade down the street."

"Who's the celebrity guest this year?" Otosan asks.

Junpei mentions a name. "He's a famous sumo wrestler."

Every year, someone famous comes to dance with the locals, and the whole thing is broadcast on national TV. Since a lot of events were cancelled this year out of respect to the victims of the tsunami, I'm surprised that the festival is being held at all. Then again, it's all about honoring the dead. Supposedly, during Obon the spirits of those who have died return for a visit. It's sort of like Mexico's Day of the Dead, which Raoul has told me about, but without the candy skulls.

"Tomorrow morning, we'll go to Kana's and Ojiichan's grave," Mariko adds.

Obaasan nods and murmurs. Her eyes even seem to twinkle. It's as if she really believes that she will meet up with her dead husband and granddaughter tomorrow.

The evening news features a ceremony farther south along the coast of Shikoku. People are gathered on a beach, sending lit candles in little paper boats out onto the waves. I hear the word "tsunami."

"Is that for the people in Tohoku?" I ask.

"No," Otosan says. "They are remembering ancestors who died in another tsunami. This one happened in Tokushima Prefecture."

"Hmmm." Eventually, it seems as if people here wind up spending more time doing things to remember the dead than they do to pay attention to the living. I can't help being glad that I live in a country where the dead don't care how the laundry is hung and how they don't go on craving cigarettes and chocolate from beyond the grave.

On the television screen a child reaches into the water and makes a joyful splash. Obaasan sucks in her breath. An adult nearby yanks the kid away from the water. What's the big deal? The water's not deep there, and the candles weren't snuffed out. The kid was just having a little fun.

"What just happened?" I ask the room at large.

"Japanese people believe that you shouldn't go in the water during Obon," Mariko says. "The spirits come up from the water and they might drag you back down with them."

That night I dream that while I'm swimming in the sea, I meet my half sister Kana. She has long flowing hair and plump cheeks. Instead of legs, she has a tail sequined with scales. Kana has become a mermaid. In the dream, I swim toward her, my arms reaching through glittering phosphorescent green. Bubbles rise from her mouth. She seems to be speaking to me, but I can't hear her. I go closer and closer and then she grabs my arm with amazing force and pulls me deeper and deeper. I wake up, gasping.

When I roll out of my futon, I find Obaasan in the kitchen making rice balls. They're for Kana, no doubt. I wonder if my grandmother dreams about the little girl, too, and if her dreams are different. I flash to an image of people standing in line for rice balls after the tsunami washed away their homes. I wonder if the people living in temporary shelters up north are making rice balls for their lost loved ones, too. And I wonder again why we can't do more for the living.

We eat a quick breakfast of miso soup, rice, and grilled salmon. At around nine o'clock, the doorbell rings. Mariko answers the door.

"The priest is here," she says.

I catch a glimpse of a middle-aged Japanese man in layered robes. He shuffles toward the shrine at the back of the house. Mariko indicates that we should all follow.

Two cane chairs have been positioned at the back of the tatami room. I take one, and Obaasan sits in the other. Junpei and Otosan kneel on cushions while

Mariko serves green tea to the priest. He slurps it down, turns to the shrine, and begins chanting. I have no idea what he's saying, but the words and the rhythm lull and soothe. Every now and then he taps the bronze bowl with a small mallet. *Ring ring.* At one point, a portable altar is passed around. I watch Mariko, in order to copy her. She pinches a bit of incense, brings it to her forehead, and sprinkles it on the altar. She does this three times.

When the altar comes to the back, Obaasan holds it on my knees while I pinch the incense and bring it to my forehead. I can hardly believe she's actually helping me. She's being nice, even if it is for the sake of Kana.

The chanting goes on for something like twenty minutes. Amazingly, Mariko, Junpei, and Otosan have been kneeling all that time. After a few final rings of the gong, the priest chats a bit with Mariko and Otosan, gathers up his robes, which must be suffocating in this heat, and makes his exit.

"Now we'll go to the cemetery," Mariko says, rising to her feet. She totters a bit, as if she's drunk. Her legs have obviously fallen asleep. "You and Obaachan can ride in the truck with me. Junpei and your father can walk."

I climb into the cab of the truck and scooch to the center of the bench seat. Mariko takes the wheel. My grandmother hauls herself in after and settles beside me. She's clutching a tangerine in one hand, and a pack of cigarettes in the other.

"How, exactly, did Grandfather die?" I ask.

"Lung cancer."

Go figure. I take another glance at the cigarettes. "Huh."

I feel around for a seatbelt, but there doesn't seem to be one. Mariko and Obaasan remain unharnessed as well, but Mariko drives turtle slow. We glide past Otosan and Junpei. The gravesite, as it turns out, is only about a hundred yards from the house. The parking lot is populated with clusters of relatives who've come to pay their respects. Mariko shifts into park and we pile out onto the pavement and wait for the guys.

Otosan issues an order. Immediately, Junpei fills up a silver bucket with water from an outdoor spigot and grabs one of the wooden ladles hanging from hooks hammered into a low stone wall. My father leads the way to the family grave. No names are engraved on the granite, but in the back there's a bundle of pieces of narrow wood carved with kanji. The ashes of deceased family members are entombed in the stone.

Otosan takes the bucket and ladle from Junpei. He dips the ladle into the water and pours it over the stones, steps back, sets the bucket down, and puts his hands together. He chants a sutra, which I don't understand at all. Next, it's Junpei's turn. I go last. I don't chant. I don't say anything out loud, but there are words in my head: "I wish I'd met you. I wish I'd known you."

Meanwhile, dragonflies dart through the air. Cottony clouds scud across the blue sky. A little girl giggles in delight.

That evening we take the train into the city along with about a million other people. The car is so crowded I can hardly move. I'm wrapped up in Sora's wisteria-patterned *yukata*. Mariko's wearing an indigo-dyed one, but Otosan and Junpei are in shorts and polo shirts. Obaasan is staying home.

"She can watch it all on TV," Mariko says.

Well, she's probably been to this event about seventy times, but for me, it's a first. I want to experience it all live and in person.

The train rattles over the bridge that spans the Yoshino River, zipping past buildings which seem too close to the tracks for comfort. Once we get off the train car, Mariko holds my arm and ushers me along. I try to keep my head above the shoulders around me. There's so much to see—flashes of colored fabric, stalls selling octopus fritters, ring toss booths, kids toting plastic bags of goldfish. I can smell corn roasting, and from everywhere, there is the jangle and beat of festival instruments.

We pick our way through the crowd until we arrive at a street lined with bleachers. Otosan hands over our tickets and a guy in a short blue *happi* jacket shows us to our seats. Junpei dashes off to buy cold drinks. Mariko reaches into her purse for a handful of folded fans and gives one to me. I flap it at my face.

A few minutes later, the first troupe comes into view, led by a trio of male musicians. One of them blows on a flute, while another drums, and yet another rings a triangle. Behind them, a sea of straw-hatted women surges forward. Arms in pink sleeves rise together. Each step is synchronized. Every now and then, they call out in unison, *"Yatto sa, yatto sa!"*

"They're so . . . coordinated," I say.

"This is one of the most famous troupes," Mariko explains. "They perform Awa Dance all over the world."

The movements are repetitive. The reaching and stepping may be simple for dancers who can control their limbs, but they must have to practice constantly to be so much in sync with one another. I'm in awe. I set down my fan and take a few photos with my phone.

Although the first group that dances past may be the most famous one, the others are not bad. They're all elegant, all adept, all utterly alive.

21

The next manga letter from Tohoku shows the young man kneeling at an altar like the one where my grandmother spends her days talking to Kana. There are framed pictures at his altar, too. His mother, his father, his grandparents, and his brother. He's drawn a broken boat. His father must have been a fisherman. In the corner, there's a baseball mitt half-buried in the mud. He must have figured out that I can't read or write Japanese because this time he signed his name in English: Kotaro Noda.

"You are not alone!" I want to write. Instead, I draw myself sitting at a table set for two. He can imagine himself entering the illustration, sitting down to tea and cake and sandwiches in a comfortable room. Away from the sea.

Now that the indigo has been processed, it's just a goopy stew that needs to be stirred every day. The hard work is over for now, so the following Saturday at lunchtime Otosan says it's time for more sightseeing.

"It would be a shame if you came all the way to Japan and you didn't see anything except for Tokushima," he says.

I nod in agreement. I would like to see a bit more and I need a distraction. I'm starting to realize that my big romance with Taiga isn't going to happen. He doesn't like me the way that I like him. I need to get over him, and I can't do that from one house away.

"Where would you like to go?" Mariko asks. "We could visit the temples of Kyoto, or drive to Mt. Fuji. We could even go to Tokyo Disneyland if you like."

I look down at my T-shirt, the one with the tulips. "Y'know, I'd love to see that fake Dutch village."

Otosan nods. "Then we'll go to Nagasaki."

The next day, my father hands me a sheet of paper. "Here is our itinerary for the weekend."

"Seriously? You made a schedule?"

It's neatly typed and very detailed. According to this, we're leaving at six a.m. Breakfast will be rice balls and cold tea, consumed in the car. At noon, we'll be stopping at a "rest station," probably like that one on Awaji Island on the way from the airport.

"We're having udon noodles?" I ask. I don't even get to pick from the menu?

"It's the local specialty," he says. "You should try it."

I've always thought that Raoul, with his color-coordinated sock drawer and alphabetized CD collection, had OCD tendencies, but this is nuts. There's no room for spontaneity or surprises.

Last summer, Mom and I just roamed around Paris, hopping into taxis at will. We stumbled over cute boutiques and off-the-beaten-track art galleries. Even though we couldn't always agree on where to eat, we had a good time. But I'm the guest here, and I really know nothing about Nagasaki, except that an atomic bomb fell on the city and killed thousands of people. I should keep my mouth shut and be gracious. And be packed and in the car at six o'clock in the morning.

In addition to Huis Ten Bosch, the fake Dutch village, I see that we'll be visiting the Peace Park and someplace called Glover House. It looks like we'll be pretty busy. There's not a lot of hanging-out-at-the-hotel time built into this schedule. I just hope that we're at each place long enough for me to make a few sketches.

I stuff some clothes, including my tulip T-shirt from Holland, Michigan, and drawing materials into the smaller of my suitcases.

* * *

Since I'll be missing this week's Skype call due to our road trip, I bring up Mom that evening. She looks calm and rested for once. Her hair is brushed and pulled back in a chignon. As far as I can tell, her shirt is unwrinkled and free of spit-up. It looks like she's even applied lipstick.

"I take it Esme's sleeping till dawn?"

"Well, not exactly. But last night was Raoul's turn."

I can't help wondering what it was like with me. "Did, uh, my father help out with me when I was a baby?"

Mom rolls her eyes. "He had no idea what to do with you. Most Japanese women go back to live with their parents the first few months after giving birth. Or at least they did back then. New dads weren't really expected to do anything, except go to work as usual."

Just as I figured.

"But, hey, he's stepping up now, isn't he? He's trying to be a dad to you now."

"Yeah, I guess." I tell her about the trip to Nagasaki, including the itinerary. "Was he always this . . . organized?"

Mom laughs. "No, not with me. I think I loosened him up a bit."

I'll bet she did. I can imagine her pulling him away from the crowd lined up outside the Eiffel

Tower down some obscure Parisian alley. Or Mom serving pancakes for dinner when Otosan was expecting fish and rice. Maybe he liked it at first, and then it got to be exhausting for him. He actually seems pretty happy with Mariko.

"Some people grow more conservative as the years go by," Mom says with a shrug.

"Lucky me," I mutter. "To meet him when he's the most uptight."

"Maybe he needs *you* to shake him up a bit. Maybe you're doing that without even trying."

I think about my early morning walkabout, when everyone panicked that I'd gone missing, and the dropped laundry that got Obaachan all discombobulated, and Junpei's trip to the principal's office. And would they have been stomping the indigo leaves in a conga line if I hadn't shown up? Yeah, I guess I'm adding a little excitement to their lives.

"What's on this agenda?" Mom asks. "What are your big plans for Nagasaki?"

I tell her about the Peace Park, and the Glover House, which I haven't gotten around to Googling yet. "Do you know anything about that?"

"Yeah, sure. Thomas Glover was supposedly the model for Captain Pinkerton."

"Captain Pinkerton?"

Mom rolls her eyes again. "Haven't I taught you anything? He's the guy in the opera *Madame Butterfly*."

"Oh, yeah. The one where the American guy hooks up with a Japanese woman, fathers her baby boy, and then leaves without marrying her." Sort of like our story, except instead of the Japanese Cho-cho-san, we've got Mom, an American, who goes back to America with her baby girl after being rejected by her Japanese Captain Pinkerton.

"That's the one. Nagasaki is a port city, so there were a lot of foreigners living there back in the 1800s."

"But the American army dropped an atomic bomb on the city anyway." People from all over the world must have died in the blast, like at the World Trade Center.

"Yes, they did," Mom says quietly.

"Oh, and we're also going to this place called Huis Ten Bosch."

Mom nods, smiling. "I remember that place! It was built while I was living there. It's a model of a Dutch village, right?"

"Like Holland, Michigan," I say.

"Well, then, you'll be right at home."

22

At five a.m., I find Mariko in the kitchen making rice balls for our trip. Or actually, they're more like triangles. I watch as she scoops a fistful of fluffy grains from the rice cooker then squeezes it between two hands.

"Can I help?"

She hesitates for a moment, her gaze landing on the stiff, curled fingers of my left hand. "Yes," she says. "Sit down at the table."

I wait while she sets her perfectly formed *onigiri* on a plate, washes her hands, and rustles through a drawer. She produces a white plastic mold and brings it over to me along with a paddle and a bowl of cooked rice. "You can use this," she says. Next, she brings some little dishes with various fillings.

Using my good hand, I scoop rice into the mold, filling it halfway. I make a depression in the center with my index finger and spoon in some tuna fish mixed with mayonnaise. Then I cover that with more rice, fit the top of the mold over it, and press down with the palm of my hand. Presto!

I shake it out onto the plate, feeling proud of myself. Mariko gives me a little nod.

By the time Obaachan appears, apparently having finished her prayers or whatever with my ghost sister, I've covered the plate with onigiri stuffed with pickled plums, fish flakes sprinkled with soy sauce, and tuna. She creeps up behind me and stabs one of the rice balls with her finger, as if testing its durability. When it doesn't fall apart, she grunts. I'll take that as a compliment.

Obaachan is not going with us on our road trip to Nagasaki. Someone has to stay and stir the *sukumo*. I'm relieved that she'll remain here. I think we both need a break from each other. Maybe while I'm gone, she'll have time to reflect. Maybe she'll come to the conclusion that I'm not such a huge threat to her family. And maybe I'll figure out a way to make her like me. Yeah, right.

Mariko and I finish the rice balls with fifteen minutes to spare. As we pack them into a plastic container, my father starts loading our suitcases into the car. Junpei finally shows his face at ten till six. He's got a serious case of bedhead, but he's dressed in a T-shirt printed with a Keith Haring dog barking at a UFO and a baggy pair of khaki cargo shorts. His muscled legs are smooth and hairless. A backpack is slung over his shoulder.

"Ready to go?" my father asks.

Junpei nods and slouches toward the car.

Mariko whips off her apron and drapes it over a chair. She's already dressed and impeccably made-up, as usual. She bundles the box of rice balls in a square of colorful cloth and hands it to me. I carry it out to the car.

Obaachan follows us as far as the porch. She doesn't hug anyone good-bye or say much of anything. I'm starting to get used to all that, but it's still so different from my American grandparents with their never-ending hugs and their smooches and endearments and jars of chocolate chip cookies. You can bet Obaachan won't be baking any treats for us while we're gone. She watches while we get into the car and bows slightly.

I look out the window as my father starts the engine. Obaachan suddenly looks smaller, standing there all alone. Maybe it's my imagination, but she seems to slump a little as we pull away. On a sudden impulse, I lift my hand and wave to her. She doesn't wave back.

Junpei pulls his iPod out of his pocket and plugs the earbuds into his ears. He falls asleep, his head lolling against the window, even before we hit the highway. I stare out the window for a while, watching the hills of pine blur by, the little towns nestled in valleys, the occasional glimpses of sea, until I fall asleep as well. When I wake up, it's nearly eight o'clock.

Mariko peers over the front seat. "Ready for breakfast?"

"Uh, yes please."

She hands me a couple of rice balls wrapped in plastic and a paper cup of hot green tea. I take a sip and settle the cup in the holder on the door. I can't tell if these are the rice balls I molded or not. I don't know what's inside until I take a bite. Tuna mayonnaise.

"Is this your first trip to Nagasaki?" I ask.

"No," Mariko says. "Your father and I—and Junpei—went there on our school trips when we were junior high students."

Otosan chuckles. "Three hundred kids together. Can you imagine?"

I shake my head. There's no way my middle school teachers would have been able to keep so many kids in line. Someone would have gone behind a dumpster to smoke cigarettes, and someone else would have left their cell phone behind and we'd have had to go back to look for it, and someone else would have smuggled beer in their luggage.

"I guess you had to be really organized," I say. Suddenly his itch to schedule everything makes sense. If one of us gets lost, all we have to do is check the itinerary.

"Yes. It was like the army. We had no privacy, no free time."

After all that, Mom must have seemed like the great liberator.

We drive and drive and drive, leaving the island of Shikoku for Kyushu, till finally we arrive in the city of Nagasaki. Mariko enters our destination—the Peace Park—into the car's navigation system. Immediately, a woman's voice begins giving directions: " . . . left . . . turn . . . straight."

Kyushu seems to be a few degrees more tropical than Shikoku. The palm trees are thicker here, their leaves more lush. Women walking along the street carry parasols and wear long gloves to shield themselves from the sun. I see a man patting a handkerchief against his forehead, sopping up the sweat. Here and there, I spot a few young foreigners, mostly backpackers.

According to my guidebook, this city was once the gateway to Japan, the only place where foreigners were allowed to enter the country. First, some Dutch explorers arrived, and there was a mania for all things from the Netherlands. This was Japan's first international city. Even though it was full of foreigners, the US Army dropped an atomic bomb here. Once, it was obliterated, like the tsunami-stricken coast of

Northeastern Japan. You'd never know it to look at it now. The buildings are new and shiny. The people are well dressed.

Otosan pulls into a parking lot.

Out of curiosity, I check the itinerary. Wow. We're only ten minutes off. We now have an hour and a half to tour the museum and park.

"Ready?" Otosan nudges Junpei, who is just waking up.

He grunts and stuffs his feet into his shoes.

We emerge from the air-conditioned car. The air is thick and moist, like soup. An orchestra of cicadas greets us. Junpei opens his eyes and stretches like a cat. I follow my father across the parking lot to the entrance of the Memorial Museum. Mariko lags behind.

Otosan goes up to the window and buys our tickets. He hands me one, along with a brochure in English, and we go inside. There are quite a few visitors milling about, some of them Americans, but the museum is library-quiet. The first room is dim and cool. Screens overhead project black-and-white images of ordinary everyday Nagasaki before the bomb was dropped. I see a photo of a girl about my age. She's wearing a sailor-collared school uniform. She isn't smiling, but she doesn't look unhappy, more like determined. Maybe she's thinking about the bright, shiny future she has ahead of herself. Thinks she has.

Against the wall, there's a brick archway flanked by statues that look like saints.

"What are those from?" I ask Mariko.

"There was a beautiful Catholic church here," she explains. "The Urakami Cathedral, one of the most magnificent in all of East Asia. It was destroyed by the atomic bomb. This is a reproduction of one of its walls."

"Wow." I think back to sitting in church with Raoul, the chanting of the priest, the tendrils of incense. Imagine being at mass, feeling all peaceful, and then having a bomb drop on you. Moving on, we come across exhibits of melted rosaries, shards of stained glass, ruined statues of angels. Why would anyone want to destroy all this? A middle-aged couple in front of me whispers in French. The woman turns to look back at me. I suddenly feel ashamed of being American. I don't want her to know that I'm from the country that's responsible for all this. I jam the English-language brochure into my pocket and vow not to speak out loud for the rest of the tour, giving my nationality away. Maybe I can pass for Japanese.

A mangled clock stopped at 11:02 hangs on the wall. That was the time, on August 9, 1945, when the bomb dropped. I silently peruse the photos taken after the bombing. The city was a wasteland, all charred and broken. In one photo, a woman drags a cart loaded with sticks. I can't imagine what they were for. Firewood? Or maybe she was going to try to build a house? More stuff: bottles melted together, a blasted helmet with the remains of a skull still inside. I see a burnt lunchbox with its contents intact. Uneaten. Then we come to a twisted water tower, which had been at the Keiho Middle School. I imagine a class-room full of kids just a couple years younger than me sitting at their desks, and then not. I stand frozen, biting my lips to keep from crying. Mariko comes up behind me. Her hand settles on my shoulder. *"Daijobu?"* she asks. Are you okay?

"Kanashi," I say. It's sad.

"It is very sad," she replies in Japanese.

In the next room, there is a glistening coppery torpedo-shaped thing, a replica of Fat Man, the bomb itself, and various exhibits urging the abolishment of nuclear weapons, just in case people haven't already gotten the message that atomic bombs are bad.

Otosan and Junpei have already reached the end of the exhibit and are waiting near the door. I guess they are familiar with all of this, especially since they've been here before.

"Do you want to write something?" Otosan asks, gesturing to a pad of paper. Some other visitors are crouched over their own pads, scribbling with pens.

One woman has just finished. She wipes a tear from the corner of her eye, folds up her paper, and tucks it into a box.

"Yeah, okay." I'm not sure what to write, though. I feel guilty even though I wasn't even alive when my two countries were at war. You could maybe even say that since I am half Japanese and half American, I am a symbol of love and peace between nations. But my parents are not together. They're not fighting each other, but they haven't reconciled either. They're still broken up. I've heard that trauma is passed along genetically. Maybe guilt is, too. On behalf of my American ancestors, I pick up the pen and write, *I'm sorry*.

Although the interior of the museum is cool and dim, it's a relief to go back into the heat and sunlight, away from the gloom.

"Shall we visit the park?" Otosan asks. It's on the itinerary. I'm not sure that he's actually giving us a choice, but I'd like to see it anyway.

"Okay." At least we'll be surrounded by trees and plants. We may have insects buzzing around our heads, but they're part of nature. They're alive.

A trail leads down the hill into a sculpture garden. The stone monuments all have some connection with the bombing. I come across one which looks like an image of hell. I can read a couple of the kanji characters carved into stone—the ones for mother and child.

I look again and guess that the bald figures with their mouths open wide are children, and the larger figures are their mothers reaching out to them. They seem to be underground, or maybe they are buried in debris. The face of a gentle-looking woman is etched into the rock above. She must be the mother of Jesus. This makes me think of the grotto at Lourdes, which Mom and I visited last summer, where Mary supposedly appeared to a girl named Bernadette. As the story goes, Mary cured Bernadette's asthma and bestowed her with healing powers. Nothing like that happened at Nagasaki, however. Not even Mary could cure all of the people who became sick due to radiation poisoning.

A brick column rises at the center of a clearing. My father stands before it, waiting for me. When I catch up with him, he looks at me and says, "This is the exact spot where the bomb was dropped."

"Ground zero."

"Yes."

I pull the brochure out of my pocket and read that the pillar is part of the Urakami Cathedral that Mariko told me about earlier. I read the plaque at the site. It says, "About one-third of Nagasaki City was destroyed and one hundred fifty thousand people killed or injured, and it was said at the time that this area would be devoid of vegetation for seventy-five years." Obviously, that last part wasn't true. There is green everywhere. But one hundred fifty thousand is a lot of people. I can't help imagining what this city would have been like if they had survived and passed on their genes. How many future artists and pop stars and robot scientists and baseball players were lost on that day? The mind boggles.

Farther on, we come to statues donated by countries around the world—Turkey, Poland. New Zealand, Italy, China, and others. Some of them are pretty straightforward—a mother lifting a baby in an expression of hope (*Hymn to Life* from Italy) and some are more abstract, like *Cloak of Peace* from New Zealand, which is a curvy silver filigreed wall. I take photos of all of them so that I can show Mom when I get back home. I wonder what kind of sculpture she would come up with if she were asked to create something for this garden. Another version of *Aiko, En Pointe*? *Father and Child*?

I note that there's another statue a little farther along of a girl who died of leukemia. It seems cruel to make Mariko and my father and Junpei walk past it. They'll be forced to think about how my sister died. It wasn't from a bomb dropped by America, but from bad luck, but still. As I'm following along behind Otosan, looking at the map and trying to figure out a detour around the statue of the sick girl, we just about run smack into it.

The bronze girl is draped with strings of colorful

origami cranes. Even though they are outside, the paper birds don't seem to have been affected by the weather. They must be new. I wonder if there are new garlands every day.

"What do the cranes mean, exactly?" I ask Mariko.

She shrugs. "Some people believe that if you fold one thousand cranes, your wish will come true. There will be peace, or your team will win the game, or your sickness will be cured. Something like that."

Sort of like praying, I guess, or going to Lourdes and hoping for a miracle. I made Mom take me to Lourdes last summer when we were in France. I didn't really expect that a visit to the grotto would make my cerebral palsy go away, but there were so many people on crutches and stretchers who looked like they desperately needed help to stay alive.

"When Kana was sick in bed, we folded paper cranes together," Mariko adds softly. "Junpei folded them, too. So did all of her classmates at school."

I hesitate for a moment. "Did you . . . make a thousand?"

She lets out a bitter laugh and reaches up to wipe her eyes. "More than a thousand."

I touch her arm lightly, urging her onward.

At the end of the park, there is a gigantic statue of a muscular man. A tour group is posing for a photo in front of him. Some of them are on risers, others crouch in front. Just then, a couple of girls in sailor-collared blouses and pleated navy skirts rush up to me. "Hello!" one of them says, flashing a mouthful of crooked teeth. "You take picture with me?"

"What?"

"They want you to pose for a photo with them," Mariko explains.

They nod. The other one, a girl with a neat ponytail and glasses, nods vigorously. "Take photo together with me!"

"Um, okay, but why me?"

The two of them giggle. "Beautiful American," they say. The girl who spoke first hands her camera to Mariko and shows her which button to push.

How can they tell I'm American? In the States, people always think I'm Asian. Once again I'm reminded that I don't blend in here as well as I thought I did. Oh, well. They are already flanking me, forming peace signs with their hands.

"Say 'peace,'" Mariko directs. She snaps a picture, then switches cameras and takes another.

"Sank you," the girls say. They reach out their hands to shake mine, giggling when our fingers touch, and then they go skipping off toward the fountain.

"That was weird," I say to Mariko.

"They were probably excited about finding someone to practice their English with. I was like that once, too."

"No way." I try to picture her, young and happy,

eagerly rushing up to some bewildered foreigner and begging for an autograph.

Otosan is way ahead of us by now. He walks too fast, and we've been delayed by these schoolgirls. I wonder vaguely if we are on schedule. According to the itinerary, we're going to the Glover House next. We meet up at the car and Otosan programs the navigation system. The chirpy woman's voice tells us to pull out of the parking lot and turn right.

The Glover House is up a steep hill. It's one story with a tile roof and a stone patio out front. Nearby, roses are in bloom. Otosan goes to the ticket booth and returns with what looks like a map and a thick pen. "Here's a talking pen," he says. "If you touch the map with it, you can hear an explanation in English."

Talking pen, huh? "Cool. Thanks."

We start the tour, Otosan and Junpei rushing ahead as usual, Mariko and me lagging behind. Although the outside of the house looks Japanese, the interior is more Western. Instead of the low tables and cushions that are in the Japanese rooms of my father's house, these rooms are filled with armchairs and fireplaces and carpets. I touch my pen to the picture of a statue of a man with a butterfly on his shoulder.

"This is a statue of Puccini, who wrote the opera *Madame Butterfly*. Many people say that the Glover House was the imaginary setting for this tragic story.

In the story, Cho-cho-san waited patiently with her child for the return of her lover, Captain Pinkerton, but he never came back. Cho-cho-san finally killed herself."

"Sort of like Mom and me," I mutter. I'm talking to myself, but Otosan has crept up beside me. He's overheard.

"Your mother was no Cho-Cho-san," he says. "And I didn't abandon her. She left me."

True. Also, Mom didn't kill herself. She brought me to America, her home country, because she thought it would be better for me. She didn't sit around pining or suffering. In fact, she pursued her dreams of being an artist and found someone else to love. Meanwhile, Otosan was stuck in Japan, unable to escape from the land and his family. Maybe, in my father's mind, he is more like Cho-cho-san, and my mother is Captain Pinkerton. Is it possible that he is still in love with her? Did he marry Mariko because she seemed like someone who'd be happy living on a farm, or did he fall in love with her, too?

With Mariko coming up beside me, I can hardly ask these questions. I touch the pen to the map again. After we've gone through all of the rooms, we go out into the garden where Junpei is tossing fish feed into a pond churning with fat orange and calico carp. Their mouths are gaping at the surface of the water.

"Wow, they look so greedy!"

"Open your hand," Junpei says. He gestures that I should cup my hand, and he dumps some of the pellets from his palm to mine.

I toss in a few. The fish lunge and swallow.

"You've been here before, right?" I can tell he's bored by this place. "Have you already been to Huis Ten Bosch, too?"

His eyes light up. "Yes, once, but I've never stayed at the new hotel. I'm looking forward to it."

What a funny kid. "What's so special about the hotel?"

"The staff members are robots!" Somehow I missed that tiny detail during our pre-trip meeting. Of course Junpei would be excited about a hotel staffed by robots. It's probably the one thing that has made this entire trip worthwhile for him. Suddenly, I'm looking forward to meeting robots as well.

In Holland, Michigan, there is a fake windmill or two and souvenir shops selling wooden shoes and Dutch-girl caps, but it's hard to forget that the rows of red tulips are not in Europe. At Huis Ten Bosch there are entire streets and canals and towering red brick buildings constructed in imitation of actual buildings in Amsterdam. If not for the Japanese words floating on the air, I'd swear that I was in the Netherlands.

The sun beats down. The back of Junpei's T-shirt

is soaked through with sweat. Mariko has pulled on white elbow-length gloves and carries a parasol.

When we check into the hotel I'm expecting a boxy metallic creature or something like R2-D2 from *Star Wars*, but the receptionist at the Robot Hotel is anything but. She's humanoid with glossy black hair that swings in a bob and glittery brown eyes. Her lifelike curves are covered with a crisp white blouse and navy skirt.

"*Irashaimase*," she says as we approach the front desk. Even her voice seems lifelike. She bows, and we bow, too. When her back is straight again, she looks right at me and adds, "Welcome."

"Whoa. How did she know that I'm a foreigner?"

"Facial recognition software," Junpei says. "It's cool, isn't it?" Suddenly he's full of energy, as if he's just mainlined a pot of coffee or something.

"Way cool." *And a little creepy.*

"May I have your name, please?" It, or she, or whatever, asks.

"Um, Aiko Cassidy. But I think the reservation is in my father's name." Let her figure that one out. Her program is probably rifling through its hard drive for some guy with the last name Cassidy.

Otosan steps up to put her out of her misery. He gives her the details in Japanese, and we are directed to our room.

"She didn't give us a key," I say to Junpei as I follow my dad and Mariko down the dimly lit corridor. The walls smell like fresh paint.

"We don't need a key," Junpei says. He's obviously read up on this place. "Just watch . . ."

When we reach our room, Otosan sticks his face up to the wall. I see that there's a sensor there. After it recognizes him the lock clicks open, and we follow him inside.

The interior is surprisingly normal—two double beds covered in white take up most of the room. There's a vaguely futuristic oval sofa in the far corner. Along one wall is a desk and a television. A large window looks out onto a panorama of tulips and windmills and tidy brick buildings.

Junpei grabs the TV's remote control and throws himself across one bed. Otosan sits on the other. So where am I supposed to sleep? I glance over at Mariko, my eyebrows raised.

"Our room is next door," she says in a low voice. "Shall we freshen up?"

"Meet us back here in fifteen minutes and we'll go eat dinner," my father calls out as we leave the room.

I feel a little shy about rooming with Mariko. After all, we're not related and she's still pretty much a stranger to me. I'd been hoping that I'd have my own room, but Mariko is kind, and maybe this will give us a chance to get to know each other better.

* * *

During dinner, in this fancy schmancy place that's decorated in the European style, and later, back in the hotel room after we've had our showers and we're watching TV, I try really, really hard not to think about Taiga. But when I pick up a brochure from the desk and glance at the list of attractions, I come across an ice skating rink and it seems like a sign. Maybe I should ask Mariko about how to deal with my feelings for Taiga.

"Mariko," I begin. "Did you ever like someone who didn't like you back?"

"What?" She lowers the volume on the TV and turns to me, clearly confused.

"When you were my age, I mean."

She clicks the TV off. For a long moment, she is silent and serene, as if enjoying a lovely memory. "Yes," she says. "There was this boy in my high school. He was in another class, but I wanted to meet him. He and I rode the same train together, every morning. I watched him. I saw what books he read. I memorized everything about him—his height, the way he parted his hair, the way he walked—but he never seemed to notice me."

"Did he have a girlfriend?" I can hardly believe he wouldn't have noticed her. I'll bet she was as graceful and beautiful back then as she is now.

Mariko shrugs. "Not that I know of. I finally

worked up the courage to speak to him, but he disappeared before I had a chance to talk to him."

"Disappeared?" Like he was kidnapped, or something? A dropout?

She sighs. "Someone told me that his family moved away suddenly. I was too late."

"Wow. That's really sad."

"No, not really," she says. "Do you know that line from a poem by Tennyson? ''Tis better to have loved and lost than never to have loved at all'?"

"Yeah, I guess."

She studies me for a moment. "Are you thinking of someone in particular? Taiga, maybe?"

Geez, am I that transparent? Does the whole world know? I bite my lip and nod.

"I think you are very special to him," she says. "He had a big shock, but for this short time, he has been able to live like a normal boy. His parents raised him expecting him to be a great skater, so he never had time to make friends or have hobbies. For him, it's usually just skating, skating, skating."

"And he'll probably go back to skating," I say darkly. I know that it has to be that way, and to be honest, I'm not so sure that skating is the only thing that keeps him from liking me in the way that I like him.

She hesitates. "Maybe you will keep in touch.

Maybe in ten years, when he is finished competing, you will still be friends. Or something more."

"Yeah, maybe."

"Or you might meet someone else. Some other guy who is just perfect for you."

"Like when you met my father?" I ask, wanting it to be true.

She smiles. "Yes, exactly like that."

The next morning, after a breakfast served up by robots in the hotel dining room, we venture out into the amusement park. In spite of the heat, there are already hundreds of people—high school couples, young families, and groups of the elderly on tour—thronging the streets.

"Let's go on the Shooting Star!" Junpei says. He's as animated as I've ever seen him. Must be those robots.

"Okay, I'll follow you." For the next few hours, I have no will of my own. I just watch as Junpei sails through the air on a zip line, not really up to trying it myself, but I go along with him into the Castle of the Dead and the Japanese Ghost Story House. Mariko and my dad mostly walk around. We catch glimpses of them window-shopping and looking at the tulips. They don't hold hands like Mom and Raoul, but they seem comfortable together. Content.

We finally meet up in late afternoon at the Ice Café. In Japanese "ice" means "ice cream," so I'm thinking I'll get a vanilla cone. But once we're inside, it's like entering an igloo. The air is chilled, and all of the tables and chairs have been carved out of big blocks of ice. Again, I can't help but think of Taiga.

Before we leave "Holland," Mariko says we must make one last stop. "We need to buy souvenirs for the neighbors."

"You go ahead," Otosan says, parking himself on a bench. "Junpei and I will wait here."

I follow Mariko inside.

The shop is well stocked with neatly stacked boxes of cookies and other confections, washcloths printed with windmills and Dick Bruna characters, key chains, and Dutch cocoa products.

Mariko fills her arms with box upon box— windmill cookies for everyone!—while I pick a few gifts for my family back home. I find a scarf printed with Van Gogh's *Starry Night* for Mom and chocolate for Raoul, who will know how to bake it into something special that we can all enjoy. I put a crisp white cap for Whitney into my basket. Maybe someday she can use it as a costume prop or as a model for one of her own creations. For myself, I choose a T-shirt imprinted with tulips, thinking that I will wear it at the next Tulip Festival in Holland, Michigan—ironically, of course. And finally, for baby Esme, I select a Miffy rabbit doll dressed in wooden shoes and a scarf. Then I remember that my other sister, Kana, was a Miffy fan. I grab another Miffy doll off the shelf to put at the family shrine.

23

When we get back to Aizumi, Mariko checks the mail. "You got another letter," she says, handing me a manila envelope. She checks the postmark. "You know someone in Tohoku?"

"Sort of." I tell her that I've been sending pictures to cheer up the refugees.

"Hmm. That's nice."

Maybe to her it's minor and silly, but this family isn't doing anything at all to help the people up north as far as I can tell. It's as if they are still consumed by their grief over Kana. They have no compassion left for others. At least I'm doing something. I open the envelope in the privacy of my room. What I see makes me smile. This time he's drawn me, the table, and himself. In this picture, we sit together and we're smiling. Outside the window there are trees and rice paddies.

Later, I call Mom.

"So how was Nagasaki?" she asks.

"Excellent." I tell her about the Peace Museum and the fake Dutch village and the robot hotel.

"Did you visit the Glover House?" she asks.

"Oh, yeah. We did." I remember how Otosan said that my mother was nothing like Madame Butterfly. "You know, I'm getting the idea that you broke my father's heart."

She frowns, but she doesn't volunteer any information.

"I always thought it was the other way around."

Mom sighs. "It was complicated. You should understand that by now. Your father wouldn't—couldn't—leave that place. If we had stayed, things would have been very difficult."

I know that she's right. My grandmother is always so bossy to Mariko, even though my father's wife is quiet and kind. Mom would have rebelled, which would have made my grandmother angry. Mom would have needed to express herself and create things with her hands. She wasn't born to be a farmer. And me? Who knows if I would have thrived? Being different in Japan isn't necessarily a good thing. Mom did what she thought was best for me, for all of us. But still, I feel a little bad for my father, and a little worried about Raoul. What if she decides that he is cramping her style? That his matching socks and alphabetized spices are all too much? What if she decides to divorce him because she thinks I don't accept him as my father?

Just then, as if he'd been reading my mind, Raoul's head appears over Mom's shoulder. "Hey, there, Aiko. We miss you! Are you having a good time?"

"Yeah," I say, weirdly relieved to find him still there. Why wouldn't he be? "I miss you, too."

The next morning, I wait until I'm alone to put the Miffy doll on the family altar. Mariko and my father have gone to the shed to check on the dye. Junpei is at school for extra classes. And my grandmother is making the rounds in the neighborhood, catching up on the gossip, I guess. It may sound stupid, but I want to have some time alone with my sister. Or her ghost. Whatever.

I kneel down on the cushion in front of the shrine and ring the bell. With the gong still resounding, I put my hands together and bow my head like I've seen the others do. I catch a whiff of oranges. Fruit is arrayed on the altar, along with a package of chocolate-covered pretzels which have probably melted by now. It seems odd, somehow, to leave junk food for the dead. Shouldn't the offerings be more nourishing? Then again, maybe in heaven no one has to worry about gaining weight or getting cavities. Maybe heaven is full of whatever a person loved in life, even if it was bad for their earthly bodies.

"So. Kana. I'm really sorry we never got to meet. I bet you were a really great kid." I pause for a moment, giving her time to conjure up some sort of sign that she's listening, like a sudden breeze or a burst of sun. Nothing happens. I can hear a cat yowling outside and the distant melodic bray of the bakery truck, but these are ordinary sounds. "We went to Nagasaki. That's why we haven't been around these past couple of days. And guess what? I got you something!" I reach around behind me and grab the plastic bag. When I reach inside to pull out the stuffed Miffy doll, it makes a loud crinkling sound.

I'm just about to set the toy on the altar when I hear footsteps in the hallway. Suddenly, my grandmother bursts into the room. I'm so startled by her presence that my left arm jerks into the altar, knocking over the incense holder and sending an orange bouncing to the floor. Uh oh. I have probably desecrated the shrine.

Obaasan's arms flap. A stream of words spews out of her. She reminds me of a coop full of disturbed chickens. I'm so surprised and overwhelmed that none of her words register. I remain frozen as she yanks the Miffy doll from my hand and throws it across the room.

"*Dete ike! Dete ike!*" she shrieks. Get out of here! Her face is flooded with red.

For a second, I'm afraid that she's going to attack me. I slink away, out of her reach, trying to formulate some sort of response. *It was an accident! I have done nothing wrong! She was my sister,* I want to say. And *I'm your granddaughter, too!* But I don't know how to put these phrases into Japanese. I don't know how to make her understand me.

She's standing in the doorway, blocking my way. I get onto my feet, ready to bolt past her, to push her aside if need be, but she grabs her head with both hands and sinks to her knees. Her mouth forms a silent *O*. Such melodrama! But no, she seems to be in pain.

"Obaasan," I say. "*Daijobu?*" *Are you okay?*

The anger is gone from her face, replaced by confusion and fear. What's happening to her? Has Kana's spirit come into the room? She falls onto the mat. I rush past her now, in search of help. I have to get to the neighbor's house! Right outside, I stumble and crash, my knee hitting the ground. My palm scrapes against concrete, but I ignore the blood and haul myself to my feet. I grab an umbrella to use as a cane and hurry as fast as I can to the house next door. "Good! Are you there?" I press the doorbell and bang on the door, but no one comes. Everyone is usually out in the fields during the day. Good must have gone somewhere with her baby.

I go back to the house and check on Obaasan. She's still crumpled on the mat, her eyes closed, but she's breathing. I could try to reach my father, but by the time he comes home it might be too late. So I grab the telephone and dial 119.

A woman answers.

"Help," I say in Japanese. "Obaasan." And then I give the address in careful syllables. *"Hayaku kite kudasai!" Please come quickly!*

The woman makes a sound of assent, but I can't be completely sure she understood. I check on my grandmother again, then go out in front of the house to try to locate a neighbor or flag down a car.

I stab out my father's cell phone number. He answers on the third ring.

"Obaasan fell down," I blurt. "I think she had a heart attack or a stroke or something. I thought I should call for help, so I did. An ambulance is on its way."

"What? Speak more slowly, please."

I take a deep breath and repeat myself. "You should come home," I say.

"Okay. We'll be there soon."

Hours seem to pass in which I go back and forth from road to room, although in reality it is only minutes before a siren pierces the morning stillness. I bend down over my grandmother again to make sure she's breathing and rush outside to stand in the middle of the road. Soon, I see the white ambulance turn onto the street, its red light whirling. I wave frantically. "*Koko!* Over here!"

The next several minutes blur by. After I direct the white-smocked medics to the back of the house, I do my best to stay out of their way. They rush past with a gurney and in no time at all, they're loading my grandmother into the back of the ambulance.

My father and Mariko show up just as the medic slams the vehicle's back door.

"It's my mother," he says in Japanese.

The medic opens the door again, and my father climbs in the back. The engine starts up and the siren blares, and then they're out of the driveway and down the road, on the way to the hospital.

I feel a hand on my shoulder. "Are you okay?"

Somehow I hadn't noticed that Mariko was standing right beside me.

"Yeah, I guess." I tell her what happened, starting with me kneeling at the family shrine, setting out the Miffy doll. "It's my fault. I upset her."

Mariko shakes her head. "You did nothing wrong. You were smart to call for help. You probably saved her life."

"But if I hadn't made her mad in the first place . . ."

Indigo Girl

I shouldn't have come to Japan at all. I should have stayed home in Michigan with Mom and Raoul and baby Esme. At least there I would have been of some use, helping take care of my sister while my parents did their work. This whole trip is turning out to be a disaster. Not only have I failed to prove myself as a farmer's daughter, I've also fallen hopelessly in love with a boy who's way out of my league and I almost killed my grandmother.

"Do you want to go to the hospital with me?" Mariko asks softly.

"Yes," I say.

Without another word, we get into the car.

On the way, we stop at school to pick up Junpei. Mariko explains what happened, leaving out the part about Miffy and me. She makes me sound like a heroine, which makes me feel even more guilty.

When we get to the Tokushima University Hospital, I recall with a start that this is where I was born. I don't remember my birth, of course, but Mom told me the name of the hospital. It's a compound of brick buildings, both old and new, at the base of Mt. Bizan. Mariko parks in a lot at the back and we go inside, past artworks encased in glass, down a corridor, then up an elevator to the Intensive Care Unit.

"Are you family?" the nurse at the reception desk asks in Japanese.

Mariko glances at me. "Yes."

The nurse buzzes us inside and shows us the procedure for visits to the ICU. First, we have to put a sterilized robe over our clothes, bonnets over our hair, and paper masks over our mouths. The nurse instructs us on the washing of hands, the changing from shoes to slippers, and the pressing of the intercom button. Finally, we are admitted to the ward.

I'm careful to steer clear of the IV poles and beeping machinery as we approach Obaasan's bed. She's wearing a pale blue hospital gown, her wispy dyed black hair splayed against the pillow. Tubes and wires snake from her veins to various monitors. Her eyes are closed, and I think she must be sleeping, but when Mariko whispers her name, her eyelids flutter open. She looks small and scared.

"Junpei is here with me," Mariko says softly. "And Aiko."

I expect her to scowl at the mention of my name, but her expression remains the same. Maybe she can't scowl because her muscles are paralyzed. Maybe she doesn't remember me and the part I played in her stroke.

As I watch the others I marvel at how just a couple of days ago Obaasan was scolding Mariko for leaving the broom in the entryway. Now she's dependent on her daughter-in-law, this woman whom she's treated like a servant for years and years. And Junpei? The eldest and only son, sole heir to the indigo? If Obaasan doesn't make it out of the hospital, he will be free of her expectations. They will all be free. Just thinking about this makes my heart beat faster, as if I've committed a crime. It's wrong to wish her dead.

"I'm sorry," I say.

Her head rolls against the pillow. I can't tell if she's refusing to accept my apology or denying the need for one. Does she even understand what we are saying? I take a seat in the corner and try to stay out of the way for the rest of our visit.

24

Later that evening, I find my father in the shed with the indigo dye. He stirs the dark goop with a long stick. The pungent aroma surrounds us. "You want to try?"

"Yeah." I take the stick from him and he steps aside. I swirl the brew, like a witch at her cauldron.

"It's alive," he says.

I know that he's referring to the bacteria breaking down the leaves during fermentation, but his words are comforting, somehow. It's better that he chose to devote himself to a living thing than just the dirt in which the plants grow.

"We have to stir it every day," he says. "We can take turns."

Easy enough. "Okay."

As I stir, I think about all of the work that went into this one vat, the planting that took place before I arrived, the weeding, cutting the leaves, and then watering them for so many days. So much labor and sweat for this color that could be just as easily produced with chemicals. That's what makes it so valuable.

Eliza Pinckney, the girl who oversaw the beginnings of indigo production in America, relied on her family's slaves to harvest and process the leaves. She didn't get dirt under her fingernails like we did this summer. She didn't work the land, so maybe she didn't love it like my father does. Maybe it was easier for her to leave.

"You can stay if you like," my father says, as if he's been reading my mind. "This place is yours, too."

I look up at him, trying to read his expression. Is he saying this now because with Mariko looking after Obaasan in the hospital he will need more help? Or is it because he is claiming me as his daughter? I want to ask him if he loves me, but I don't dare. What if he hesitated? What if he only said the words because he knew that they were the ones I wanted to hear? So instead, I ask him another question. "Why did you tell the school that I was Junpei's cousin? Why didn't you tell them that I was your daughter?"

He takes a step back and stumbles. A look of despair sweeps across his face. So it's true. It wasn't a case of miscommunication or my misunderstanding. He really did lie about my relationship to him. I guess he figured that I wouldn't understand the Japanese, that I would be oblivious to his deceit. Well, at least he's not denying it now.

"This area is very conservative," he says. "It's not like America, where anything goes. Being born to parents who aren't married is still considered shameful here."

I nod, but my jaw is clenched.

"We didn't want people to think badly of you, to think that you meant less to us because you lived abroad," he continues softly. "We didn't want you to lose face."

To my great shame, a tear slips out of my eye and into the vat.

"But I see that that was wrong."

"I don't care about all that," I say with a sniffle. "Not having a dad has always been the least of my worries." Well, that's not exactly true, but when I walked up on that school stage, probably everyone was looking at me and thinking "foreigner" and "crippled," not "bastard."

"If you like, I can meet with the principal and make an announcement."

"Seriously?" Could he be bluffing? And how weird would that be, to have the whole school assemble so that everyone could hear the news that, hey, I'm not Junpei's "*itoko*," I'm actually his "*o-nesan*"? I can leave whenever I want to, but my father and his family are here to stay. Whatever scandals erupt, they're the ones who'd have to live with the aftermath. "But you would lose face."

He nods solemnly. "It's okay. I don't mind." If I asked, right about now he'd probably rip his gut open with a sword to show his penance.

It occurs to me that the indigo and tradition really are important to him. All this time I thought it was fear and obedience, but there's more to it than that. Even if Obaasan never comes home from the hospital, he will keep tending this land. He'll continue after I leave, with or without Junpei's help. It will take more than a tarnished reputation to make him stop.

"No," I say, as firmly as I can manage. "That won't be necessary." *Just tell me that you love me, your oldest daughter, and we'll be square.* "Besides, I think the neighbors have figured it out already."

"Yes," he says quietly. "Many people here remember your mother. And they remember you."

25

In the days that follow, I help out as well as I can with housework and the indigo. I bring tea and rice to the family altar every morning for Kana and my grandfather, former Living National Treasure. I'm so busy that I hardly notice that my summer vacation is ticking away. Then I get a text message from Sora: "Let's do cosplay before you leave!"

"???"

"There's a festival called Machi Asobi. Town Play. Happens this weekend! Everyone wears a costume!"

Well, I did bring a wig for just this occasion. And it would be the ultimate vacation memory to go to a cosplay event in Japan. But if Otosan and Mariko need me at home, of course I won't go.

While I'm helping to wash the rice for dinner, I ask Mariko what she thinks.

"Of course you should go!" Her voice is unnaturally bright. She's been at the hospital all day. She must be worn out. "You should have fun while you're here."

"Thanks," I reply in a low voice.

"Can you invite Junpei?" Sora texts later.

"Sure."

"And I'll invite Taiga." She adds a winking emoticon.

I blush, glad that she can't see. I know that we have no future, that he will go back to skating and I will go back to America, and that I have promised myself that I will try to get over him, but I do want to see him again. Just once. I hope he says yes.

It takes some doing, but I finally persuade Junpei to go along.

"No costume," he says.

"That's fine. I'm sure they won't mind. We'll just say that you're my chaperone."

He nods, satisfied.

"Though maybe you could wear an eyepatch or something. That would be okay, right?" He could dress up at Black Jack, the rogue doctor from the Tezuka comic. We could put a wig on him, and a lab coat.

"No costume!"

"Okay, okay."

On Saturday morning, we take the bus to the station. I'm wearing my wig and outfit. I spot Sora in her candy-apple red wig from the bus window. And there's someone tall and lanky in a maid outfit and blonde sausage curls. Can it be who I think it is? We get off the bus and cross the street. Someone shoves a packet of tissues at me with a promotional message tucked inside. There's a foreign guy in an aloha shirt playing a guitar, an overturned sombrero on the sidewalk in front of him. The manga club members are waiting just beyond him, in front of Starbucks.

Sora squeals a greeting. My gaze goes to the maid outfit, the golden curls—Taiga in drag. "Hey, you look good as a girl," I say. And he really does. His features are just delicate enough to be feminine. No one will know that a famous skater is in their midst. "Great disguise."

"Thanks," he says, striking a pose. "I haven't dressed up like this since my high school culture festival."

I raise my eyebrows. "It's a thing here?"

"Haven't you watched Japanese TV?" Sora asks. "Boys always put on girls' clothes!"

"So maybe I should have dressed up as a guy." I pluck doubtfully at a strand of wig.

"Like Takarazuka!"

"What's that?"

"It's a theater where all of the parts are played by women. Romeo and Juliet, Rhett and Scarlett, Lady

Oscar and Andre. Many love stories, all women. Next time you come to Japan, I'll take you there."

"Thanks." Maybe I won't leave at all. Every time I think of getting back on the plane, I'm seized with panic. Obaasan is still in the hospital because of me, so I should stay here and help. And part of me wants to hang out more with Taiga even if he isn't in love with me. And I think that Junpei could use a big sister. And then there's Sora and her crew. How can it be that just when I'm finding my place, it's almost time to go back?

Honestly, it's still a bit too hot for cosplay. Instead of wearing this wig, I should have my hair gathered up in a ponytail. Instead of this pseudo-paratrooper outfit, I should be wearing a sundress. I wish I could dump a handful of ice cubes down the front of my shirt.

"I love your costume," Sora says. "Who are you?" Sora, in her red wig and gray junior high school uniform, is dressed up as Kayano Kaede from *Assassination Classroom*. She carries a fake plastic rifle for added effect.

I pull a screwdriver out of one of my cargo pockets and a can opener out of another.

"She's Gadget Girl," Taiga says.

"Oh! I understand!" Sora declares. "And Junpei is Black Jack! Good costume."

I finally got him to give in with the argument

that he would stand out more at a cosplay event if he didn't dress up at all. His wig is half black, half white. The hair falls into his face, and he's wearing a surgical mask over his mouth so no one will be likely to recognize him. The rest of his costume is a white lab coat and a swath of foundation slightly darker than his natural skin color across one side of his face. As a child, Black Jack, the doctor from the Tezuka manga, received a skin graft from his best friend, who is half-African. He was injured in an explosion, and he spent many years in a wheelchair but overcame many obstacles and became a great doctor. Anyway, that's the reason for the two-toned skin.

"First, let's go to Poppogai for the cosplay competition," Sora says. "Follow me."

Poppogai is a covered shopping street near the station. It also seems to be cosplay central. Already there are a lot of people in various wigs and costumes milling about. Some are striking poses and taking photos of each other with their cell phones.

Junpei hangs back, but I grab his arm and pull him forward. "Sora looks pretty cute today, don't you think?"

He blushes and shrugs. *"Shiran."* I don't know.

We work our way to the makeshift stage and watch as people dressed up in homemade costumes show them off. All of us are too shy to compete, but we take photos of each other.

"Can you take a picture of me with Taiga?" I ask Sora.

He shakes his head and waves his hands, laughing.

"Oh, c'mon. I don't have any photos of you." Sure, I could download something from the Internet like one of his official skating photos, but it's just occurred to me that I don't have any to prove how special he has been to me this summer. Nothing to help me through the long cold winter in Michigan that's sure to come. I get the feeling that no one else has ever seen him in drag.

"Okay, but no sharing," he says. He steps up next to me and slings an arm over my shoulder—so very un-Japanese, but I'm not getting any romantic vibes.

Sora brings my phone to her eyes. "Ready? Say *chee-zu!*"

Taiga holds up two fingers in a peace sign.

Sora snaps the shutter, and this moment is saved for posterity.

Later, we venture toward the boardwalk alongside the river that runs through the city. There we find hordes of people flocking towards famous voice actors and manga artists who sit behind tables, signing autographs. I spot several other Kayano Kaede characters and another Black Jack or two. I'm the one and only Gadget Girl.

We buy cups of shaved ice drizzled in syrup in primary colors as bright as our wigs and sit by the water. To my left, I notice that Sora and Junpei are actually having a conversation. Suddenly I have hope for Junpei. Maybe he won't be spending his life pretending with pretty robots after all. Maybe he will actually find a flesh and blood girl to fall in love with, someone like Sora. When I catch her eye, I wink. She discreetly winks back.

By the time we get off the bus at home, we're all sweaty and tired. Junpei has already taken off his mop of hair and lab coat, but I urge Taiga to leave his costume on. "Just come inside for a sec. Mariko will get a kick out of seeing your costume," I say.

We step inside and shuck our shoes, barely noticing that a new, unfamiliar pair is lined up in the entryway. I pull Taiga into the kitchen, and then I freeze.

Otosan and Mariko are sitting at the table. They're not alone. A guy I've never seen before is at Junpei's usual place, a cup of tea in front of him. He's young, in his late teens or early twenties, I think, and he's gorgeous. He has shoulder-length hair and hollowed-out cheeks, and large, soulful eyes. There's an air of melancholy about him. He acknowledges our entrance with the slightest of nods, the barest of smiles, but he seems more sad than cold.

We have obviously walked in on something intense and private. I glance at Taiga, wanting to push him out of the room—get us both out of here. His eyes are fixed on the stranger. In them I see a mixture of shame and longing, that same look that I saw in Otosan's eyes when he accidentally saw my mother via webcam. Suddenly, I know the reason that Taiga has never treated me like more than a friend, more than a sister. He has never looked at me the way he is looking at that guy.

Before I have a chance to introduce him, Taiga lowers his eyes, yanks off the wig, and mutters an apology. He bows and steps back, through the threshold and to the entryway. I follow him out.

"Sorry about that. I didn't know they had company," I tell him in a low voice.

"Don't worry about it." He tugs on a curl of my wig. "Thanks for inviting me along today. I'll see you later."

After he's left, Otosan comes into the hallway. He doesn't look happy. He's holding an envelope with my handwriting. "This boy says that you've been writing to him and you invited him to our house."

"What?" Then it dawns on me. The table set for two, the empty chair filled by my pen pal. That's Kotaro in there! "I guess . . . I didn't realize that I had invited him, but maybe I did." Even as I babble I realize that I really did mean it as an invitation. Deep down, I really was hoping he would come here. And now he has! "Um, yes, I did. Obaasan is in the hospital and Junpei doesn't want to be a farmer. Think about it! You need help, that boy needs a home. I thought it was the right thing to do." I start out strong, but my spiel peters into a whisper under his harsh gaze.

"No," he says. "It was not the right thing to do. You had no business doing such a thing. You are not the head of this family. And now you have made a big mess."

"I-I'm sorry."

And I *am* sorry. Very sorry. But what does he want me to do? Tell the guy to go back to Tohoku? Should I offer to apologize and tell him that it was a hoax? Or maybe bring him back to America with me? I could appeal to Raoul's sense of Christian charity and Mom's do-gooder side. Maybe he could work as an assistant to my mother? Teach Japanese at the community college? Become Esme's nanny?

Otosan interrupts my thoughts. "Go and put on different clothes and join us," he says, frowning at my costume. "We will discuss together."

26

I quickly scrub the makeup from my face and change into jeans and my tulip T-shirt. I'm suddenly a bundle of regrets. If only I hadn't tried to put the Miffy doll on the family shrine! If only I hadn't lured Kotaro to my father's house! If only I hadn't come to Japan!

This time I bow when I enter the room and ask to be excused for my rudeness. Junpei has already joined them. He looks up at me, worried. I catch Mariko's sympathetic glance and sit down at the table next to my father, who introduces me in Japanese. I catch the word *"chojo"*—"eldest daughter."

"Kotaro Noda," the guy says, giving his name. *"Yoroshiku onegai shimasu."*

"I'm Aiko," I say.

Is it my imagination, or does he suddenly look a bit relieved?

I notice the duffle bag against the wall and wonder if that's all that was left to him after the wave. I have a vision of him going from house to house with that bag slung over his shoulder, looking for a place to stay.

My father says something about a youth hostel and Mariko says, "Sunshine Inn." I glance over at Kotaro and imagine him all alone in some strange hotel room. Poor guy.

"He can sleep in my room," I blurt out in English. "I can sleep in Obaasan's room, or in front of the shrine. With Kana."

I see a flicker of interest in Kotaro's eyes. He doesn't seem to understand much English, but I'm sure that he can tell by my tone and my father's stunned expression that I just said something outrageous. Mariko presses her palm to her mouth as if signaling me to stop speaking. Otosan shakes his head nearly imperceptibly. Junpei is staring at the table.

My father likes for everything to be planned well in advance. Having a stranger show up on his doorstep is something that he would have never imagined. And yet, sixteen or so years ago, he went to Paris and fell in love with my mother. It must have been spontaneous and surprising, and maybe it didn't turn out as well as they expected, but they were happy for a while. At any rate, my very existence proves that he was once capable of acting on impulse and doing something straight from the heart.

Let him stay, at least for the night. I beam a telepathic message to my father. *Do the right thing.*

Finally, he takes a deep breath and says to Kotaro in Japanese, "You should rest. You've had a long journey."

Kotaro is still there at dinnertime. He's sitting in a chair by the window, looking outside. Although I want to go over and talk to him, reassure him somehow, he looks like he wants to be left alone, so I volunteer to help Mariko in the kitchen.

"Can you shuck this corn?" she asks me, nodding to a pile of ears. "We'll have a barbecue tonight."

"Sure!" I get straight to work, weighing a cob down with a heavy cutting board, and then peeling back the green leaves and the strands of silk with one hand. My method takes time, but it works.

I catch some movement out of the corner of my eye and turn to see Kotaro beside me. Without speaking, he reaches for a corncob and carefully pulls back the leaves. I glance at Mariko, trying to communicate with my raised eyebrows. *See? He's helpful!* She nods slightly, but she doesn't say anything.

I put the first ear of corn in a colander and start on the second. We prepare wedges of pumpkin and strips of green pepper while Otosan fires up a grill outside on the patio. When the coals are ready, Mariko calls out for Junpei to come to dinner.

We sit in lawn chairs around the grill, turning over thin slices of meat and then dipping them and the charred vegetables into small dishes of tangy sauce.

With a combination of Google Translate and gestures and Japlish, I learn how Kotaro got a ride out of the disaster region with a volunteer group and later took a bus and a train to get here. He wanted to be far away from the sadness, he says. He wanted to see if it was possible to forget.

"Is it?" I ask him.

He shakes his head. "No. But maybe I begin again. Something new."

I see that he has an appetite. I wonder if he's been subsisting on rice balls in the shelter. I wonder if he's worried about what will happen tomorrow, like I am. Every now and then, he looks over at me. When I catch his eye, I smile.

"Is this your first visit to Shikoku?" I ask him in Japanese.

He nods. "Very beautiful. Much nature."

As if on cue, a little green frog hops on by.

Otosan avoids looking at me throughout the meal. Maybe he is thinking about how he will send this broken young man away.

27

After dinner, I help with the dishes. We take turns going into the bath. Kotaro goes first, because he is the guest.

I decide to hang out in my room and stay out of everyone's way. I try to do some drawing, but there's too much chaos in my head. My thoughts carom between Taiga in that wig and dress, the shock of finding Kotaro at the table, Otosan's anger, and Junpei's misery. I need to do something positive, something helpful. Maybe I can do something for Obaasan.

I don't really feel like going into this whole mess with Mom, so I dash off a quick message asking her to send a video of me as a child at physical therapy—a clip of me falling down and getting up again. Then, I give in to fatigue and sprawl across the futon. Next thing I know, it's morning.

★ ★ ★

I check my mailbox. Sure enough, there's a message from Mom with a file attached.

When I've washed my face and dressed in shorts and a T-shirt, I find Kotaro at the kitchen table again with Otosan and Junpei. They are looking through a magazine called *Hot Pepper*.

I picture the three guys preparing a Mexican meal together. "Is that a cooking magazine?" I ask Mariko in a low voice.

She's at the stove ladling rice and soup into bowls. "What? Oh, no. It has job listings."

Otosan asks Kotaro something about a forklift. Kotaro shakes his head. He was a fisherman. I think he would be happiest working outside, not in some warehouse.

Almost as soon as we've eaten and cleaned up, Mariko is out the door, on the way to the hospital to sit with Obaasan. Junpei retreats to his room and his robots. I crank up my laptop and get busy.

I've got three video clips—me, as a little kid struggling to walk; Taiga, crashing into another figure skater on ice and recovering enough to win a medal; and baby Chika taking her first steps. I splice them together, then add a soundtrack—"Tubthumping," an old song by this British group called Chumbawamba. After a bit more editing, I've got a short film sure to inspire the grumpiest granny. It even brings tears to my eyes.

232

* * *

The next morning, I follow Mariko into the hospital room, my laptop tucked under one arm. Obaasan looks tiny, adrift in white sheets. Her eyes are closed when we enter.

"Obaachan," Mariko says. "Aiko is here." She motions for me to approach the bed.

With what seems to be extreme effort, my grand-mother opens her eyes. She seems scared—of me?—and I suddenly can't believe I was ever frightened of her myself.

"Hello," I say, settling in the chair beside the bed. "I brought something to show you."

I set up the laptop on the hospital table. Mariko positions Obaasan so that she can see the screen well.

"Okay, so first, Mom sent along some photos from when I was little." Mariko translates my words into Japanese as I narrate the slideshow. Here's me on my first day of kindergarten. Here's me playing in the snow. Here's me at my best friend's birthday party, and so on. Every now and then, I check to see if my grandmother is actually paying attention. And every time I glance at her, expecting to find that she's averted her eyes or fixed a scowl upon her face, I find that she is actually interested in these images of my life.

Finally, I plug a USB stick into the side of the computer. "And I made this video for you."

Mariko leans closer. She hasn't seen it yet either. When the music starts up, it's a little too loud so I turn it down. Both of them stare at the screen, waiting. Suddenly, there's three-year-old me, with my brown hair held back with barrettes shaped like puppies. At first the camera hones in on my face, the eyes I got from my father, the nose from Mom. Next, the angle widens and we can see the brown hands holding me up. My pudgy right fist is wrapped around a bar. My other arm jerks uselessly at my side. The therapist, a young African-American woman with cornrowed hair, tells me to go to my mother, who sits on her knees with her arms outstretched. I let go of the bar. The brown hands release me, and there I am, taking my first awkward steps and falling and trying again.

I glance over at Mariko and my grandmother. Their eyes are glistening with tears. The image dissolves and Taiga appears on the screen in a practice leotard, spinning and crashing to the ice. He brushes the ice crystals from his hips, loosens up his shoulders, and takes off again. And there's Chika, standing in a sea of indigo leaves, looking surprised at her own accomplishment. "Da! Da!" she says, toddling forward into the arms of Good.

"This is for motivation," I say. "When I come back here next year, I expect to see you on your feet. *Ganbare!*"

Mariko's translation isn't quite so bossy, but I can tell that Obaasan gets the idea. She reaches out, her hand flailing for a moment before she latches onto mine. *"Yoi ko,"* she rasps.

"You're a good girl," Mariko translates. "She's saying 'thank you.'"

28

Otosan has not spoken to me for three days. This must be that Japanese pride Mom is always telling me about. The importance of not losing face. I don't want to go back to America with my father mad at me. I realize that it's up to me to make things right between us. It's hard to catch him alone, though. After dinner, we no longer watch the TV news because it might upset our guest. Otosan drinks beer with Kotaro at the table and they talk about farming. I linger, waiting to be noticed, but when Otosan doesn't even bother to look my way, I go to my room to sketch and send text messages.

On the fourth evening, after the dishes are washed, I walk up to Otosan and say, "Can I talk to you?"

He looks up at me, seemingly surprised at my boldness. When he glances over at Kotaro, he gets a nod of encouragement. Kotaro rises and leaves us alone.

"Can we go outside and sit on the steps?" The night is cool for once, the sky all starry.

Otosan grunts and eases out of his chair, leaving his freshly poured beer behind. I sit on the front step. Otosan lights a mosquito coil before sitting down beside me. He gazes into the murky bushes at the edge of the property and waits.

"I-I w-wanted to say that I'm sorry for all the trouble I caused," I begin. My heart is flopping around like a fish. I take a deep breath to settle myself. "But maybe Kotaro could stay here and help you. You know, Junpei doesn't want to be an indigo farmer. His dream is to design robots."

His nostrils flare, and I expect him to lash out at me, tell me that I don't know what I'm talking about, but deep down he must know how his son feels. I quickly add, "I'm so grateful for everything that you have taught me about indigo this summer. I really wish I could take over the farm."

He nods, his jaw still clenched.

"But I can't. Mom needs me, too. I promise I'll take everything I learned back with me, though. In fact, I've already decided that I'm going to try to grow a patch of indigo back home in Michigan."

I pause, giving him a chance to speak, but he says nothing. All we hear is a chorus of frogs coming from a nearby rice paddy.

His silence is driving me nuts. Isn't there

anything that I can say to get a rise out of him? Doesn't he care?

"There's another thing I should tell you," I blurt. "My stepfather wants to adopt me."

Otosan's breath seems to stop.

"I've decided that I want to go through with it. I want to be his legal daughter." Having said it, I realize that it's true. I don't want to be the odd one out in my brand-new American family. I've never had a real family before, or a father. Pretty soon I'll be leaving home, but I want to know what it's like, even if it's only for a short time.

I wait for him to start in about how they need me as well—to take over the farm and heal their grief, but he doesn't say anything. He just nods while staring straight ahead.

Finally, desperately, I throw my arms around him. "You're my family, too. I want to come back next summer. If you'll have me."

At first, he stiffens in my arms, not used to hugs or emotions, but then he seems to remember what it means to love an American and he pats me on the back. "Of course we'll have you."

29

A week before I leave, we're having breakfast and Otosan says, "Would you like to invite your friends over for a sayonara party? Maybe a dying party?"

"Wha-a-at?" Haven't we had enough of dying? Do we need to keep reminding each other? I glance over at Kotaro, who is concentrating on shoveling rice into his mouth. Maybe he didn't hear, which is just as well.

Otosan persists. "Well, now that the indigo is ready, don't you want to dye some cloth to take back home with you?"

"Oh." Of course. "Yeah, that would be great."

I invite Sora and the other members of the manga club. I send a text to Taiga. They all reply that they will come.

On the morning of the party, we gather in the shed. Mariko sets up equipment for batik, and Junpei spreads a blue tarp across the cement floor. Otosan strings up a clothesline so that we can dry our creations. I watch as Kotaro stirs the brew. He's a natural. He looks up at me, his face still and serious.

"*Kusai, desu yo?*" I say, wrinkling my nose.

He shakes his head slowly. "I like the smell."

As my eyes follow the movement of his arm, the swirl of the dye, I imagine him next year, and the year after, here in the shed. I picture him happy. Smiling.

"I'll keep writing to you," I say, miming drawing a picture. "After I go back to the States."

He does smile then, a little. It's just a brief tug at the corners of his mouth. "Okay."

The quiet is shattered by the clop of boots and the tinkle of laughter. Sora and a few other manga club members show up at the shed with squares of white cotton. She hands over a pink bakery box. "We can have cake after," she says.

"Thanks." I give the box to Junpei who takes it inside the house for now.

"Does anyone want to do batik?" Mariko asks in Japanese. She's prepared wax on the sidelines.

"I do!" Sora says. "I want to make a manga handkerchief." She shakes out her cloth and I see that she's already drawn a face with saucer eyes and spiky hair in pencil.

"Me, too!" Saho's design is more complicated, showing a figure in a ruffled dress holding a parasol. Yuma has drawn a ninja on his handkerchief.

"Shall we get started then?" Mariko says.

I check the door. Taiga's not here yet. Maybe something came up. Or could it be that he's embarrassed about seeing Kotaro again after appearing that first time in drag? I dig my cell phone out of my pocket. There are no new texts.

"What are you dyeing?" Sora asks me, bouncy as usual.

"I think I'll start with a scarf for my mother. And then a onesie for my baby sister, Esme."

I watch as Mariko applies melted wax to cloth with a special tool. She also shows us how to make different designs by gathering up cloth with rubber hands. With one hand, the wax would be easier, but I want to make stripes.

"Do you want some help?" Mariko asks me.

"No, I can do it." If I can manage a ponytail, I can do this. I sit at the table and lean my left elbow on the scarf. I work a rubber band onto the knuckles of my right hand, grab a bit of cloth, twist it, and ease the rubber band over the bundle.

I'm working on the third bundle when I feel a presence behind me.

"Hi. Sorry I'm late."

I turn, and he is there. Taiga, tall and strong and holding a white T-shirt. My heart leaps like a flying fish. *If I never saw you again, live and in person, I would have collapsed in misery*, I want to blurt out. Instead, I say, "Thank you for coming."

He shrugs. "I wouldn't have missed it."

Today there is no music mix, only the last cicadas of summer. Out of deference to Kotaro, who is still in mourning, after all, this occasion is less party than ritual. When we're ready to dye, we all gather around the vat and take turns dipping our cloths. We dip once, twice, three times, more, until we have the shades of blue we desire. Mariko pins our works to the clothesline. They ripple in the breeze like Tibetan prayer flags.

After the dyeing, Junpei brings back the cake on a tray with plates and forks, and Mariko brings cold barley tea. We eat and talk at the table and take photos of each other on our cell phones so that we can remember this day: Sora and me, the manga club and me, Kotaro and Junpei and Taiga, and every other possible combination. Sora and the others have to catch a bus and go to cram school, so they leave first. Before they go, we all hug and make promises to stay in touch.

"Come back next year!" Sora says. "We can do cosplay again!"

"I will!"

Taiga stays behind. We sit at the table in the shed talking, until after everyone else—Mariko, Otosan, Junpei, and Kotaro—has gone back into the house.

Taiga pulls his iPod out of his pocket. "Listen," he says, reaching across the table and plugging the earbuds into my ears. I hear brass and timpani, a sax melody winding like smoke—the climax of "Rhapsody in Blue."

I cock my head. "I've converted you to Gershwin?"

"This is going to be the music for my next program. I've already told my choreographer that it has to be this. I've even worked out a few moves on my own." He gives me a long look, and I realize he's waiting for me to soak up the significance of this moment, to say something meaningful in return.

"I'm so glad you're going back to skating," I say, even though a part of me wants him to stay in Tokushima so that he'll be here when I come back. But that's so selfish of me. "The people of Tohoku need you."

Actually, the whole world needs him.

"I'll think of you every time I skate to it," he says. "This summer, with you, has been really great."

I wish I could take his words and preserve them in amber. I wish I could wear them on a chain around my neck, or at least get him to repeat himself into my smart phone so I can listen over and over when he is no longer next to me. Then again, that's not really necessary. It's not as if I will ever forget.

It seems like here in Japan, in my father's family especially, so much goes unsaid. But I want my thoughts and feelings to be known. I want Taiga to know what he has been, what he is to me. I summon all of my courage, look into his gentle eyes and say, "Taiga, I love you."

He looks surprised for a moment, and then sad, and I wonder if anyone has ever said those words to him before. Maybe they feel like a trap, an obligation. I lean back. See? No strings attached. I don't want him to feel that he has to come up with an excuse or an apology for not feeling the same.

But then his face crinkles into a smile and he says, "I love you, too." He stands up and throws his arms open. I step into them. His arms, so full of grace, are actually very strong, and my face mashes against his shoulder. It's a brotherly hug, a "just friends" hug, not exactly the kind that I want but I'll take it just the same.

"If you happen to catch a skating competition on TV, watch me in the Kiss and Cry," he says, "You know, the little booth where the skaters wait to hear their results. I'll say your name."

"Okay." I bite my lip, willing myself not to bawl. I'm trying not to think about how he will go back up north, back into his life as an international celebrity, forever out of reach. I will be one of the hundreds—no, thousands—of people whose lives he has touched—a groupie, a fan girl, one who barely knows the definition of "salchow."

"Well," he says, making a move toward the door. "I guess this is it."

My heart stutters. "Wait!" I want him to have something to remember me by, something more personal and concrete than a song on his iPod. I hurry to my room and grab my sketchbook. I carefully tear out the best sketch I've made of him, write my signature in the corner, and hand it to him.

He accepts it with both hands and a bow. *"Domo arigatou gozaimashita."*

I do my best to bow back, but it feels so awkward. I guess I should send him off with *"sayonara,"* but it seems too final. *"Mata ne,"* I say instead.

He grins and returns the greeting in English: "See you again."

30

At the airport, I hug them all. In my arm, Junpei feels like a bundle of sticks, all stiff and straight. "Come and visit me in Michigan, okay?" I tell him loud enough for Mariko and my father to hear. It's never too early to plant the idea in their heads, to get them thinking about letting Junpei go out into the world. "I'm sure Raoul would be happy to have another guy around the house for a week or two."

Next, I huddle against my father. "Thanks for everything."

He pats me on the back. "Thank you for your help."

Finally, Mariko. She folds me into her arms and we melt into each other without saying anything at all. When she releases me, she wipes her eye with a finger. "We're so glad you came. Have a safe trip!"

And then I'm in the sky again, above the clouds. Between Japan and America, the past and the future. Miles and miles, hours and hours later, I gather my bags and go into the arrivals lounge and there they are. They're not holding a sign, but why would they be? I know them.

Mom comes running at me. "Oh, my baby, I missed you so much!"

"Hi, Mom," I say. "I missed you, too."

Raoul appears behind her, baby Esme in his arms. She's grown some, but when I reach out my finger she grabs on as if she remembers me.

"Esme!" I plant my lips on her perfect plump cheek.

At last, I turn to Raoul, my kind, steadfast, tidy stepfather. Something like hope radiates from his eyes. "Dad," I say, calling him that for the first time. "I'm home."

acknowledgments

Many thanks to my fellow students in the UBC Optional Residency MFA Program, and my thesis advisor Maggie de Vries, and additional thesis committee members Annabel Lyon and Linda Svendsen. This book is so much better because of you. Thanks also to SCBWI for early encouragement via a Multicultural Work-in-Progress grant, to my fellow SCBWI members in Japan, and to writer friends Ona Gritz and Helene Dunbar for commenting on drafts. Also, thanks to Trish O'Hare, Sasha Grossman, Caron Knauer, Carrie Pestritto, and to Yuzuru Hanyu for inspiration.

about the author

Suzanne Kamata was born and raised in Grand Haven, Michigan, and later moved to South Carolina where she graduated from the University of South Carolina. She came to Japan on the JET Program in 1988. She has previously published eleven books, including the young adult novels *Gadget Girl: The Art of Being Invisible* (GemmaMedia, 2013), which won the APALA Honor Award and was named a Book of Outstanding Merit by Bank Street College; and *Screaming Divas* (Simon Pulse, 2014) which was named to the ALA Rainbow List. She has also received awards from the Sustainable Arts Foundation, Independent Publisher, SCBWI, and Half the World Global Literati Award, among others. Additionally, her stories and poems for young people have appeared in *Cricket*, *Cicada*, *Hunger Mountain*, *YARN*, and the anthology *Tomo: Friendship through Fiction: An Anthology of Japan Teen Stories*. She has an MFA from the University of British Columbia and is an associate professor at Naruto University of Education in Japan. She lives with her husband in Aizumi on the island of Shikoku.

CPSIA information can be obtained
at www.ICGtesting.com
Printed in the USA
LVHW012027040719
623150LV00002B/408